ANGEL OF REALITY

And Other Unorthodox Encounters

ANGEL OF REALITY

And Other Unorthodox Encounters

DEDICATION

TO JILL, who shaped my reality in ways I did not imagine.

And I can imagine pretty well.

ACKNOWLEDGEMENTS

I HAVE HAD THE UNIQUE PLEASURE to be alive during a period of time of what I believe is unparalleled creative output. Of All the Unorthodox Beings I have been privileged to encounter, all the books, music, movies, and all the varied ways and paths of storytelling available in this, our oft-times troubled age, all of it brings us the opportunity to shift and alter our perceptions and maybe release the old and seek the new.

May our collective future be a time of growing harmony with all of earthly life.

Thank you to all who have gone before seeking peace. Thank you to all who are just arriving.

Welcome to Earth.

Author's Notes

I USED TO BELIEVE that people were looking at me askew. Turns out that the askew-ity was more from my point of view. Long held traditions traditionally look like targets for my own brand of irreverent observation. Long held rules that people accept as normal usually end with a question mark for me. The curse is that I can often see the alternate point of view as an equally viable option.

This does not imply my agreement with the alteration. I often need to remind folks that I am not actually proselytizing a new doctrine. Evangelizing is not my bag. I rarely feel the need to sway people to my way of thinking. It is a moving target anyway.

Except. I believe that a story should make the reader feel better about themselves. A reader should feel there are more options to their lives. I believe that a story should be thought provoking.

I believe stories help us to examine long held beliefs and ask whether they are still valid. It is up to the individual reader to decide if they will then abandon archaic beliefs and choose a bolder path of individuality.

Most people find comfort in the sameness of life and thus are challenged when a story deviates from familiar tropes. Hollywood makes tons of money by re-working the same scripts every year. Publishing houses create trends and adhere to strict genres so that consumers know what to buy without having to give too much thought to the decision. Similar cover design? Similar storyline.

Life is hard. Stories are an escape for most folks. Formula allows ease of access to the escapiness aspect. I myself enjoy reading the same stories again and again. Author Gene Wolfe once said that his definition of a good story is one that can be read again and again where the reader gains something new with each consecutive pass. That kind of writing requires a great degree of thought on the part of the author. It is difficult. That is why it is rare.

Genre work is fun. It is essentially reading the same story over again, just with a not-too-different cover, title, and main characters with different names. Unless it is a series.

Genre is an easily definable categorization of a work. Like Mystery or Romance or Science Fiction. You know what to expect from those.

For the writer it is enjoyable to plot and re-configure their characters' actions in an attempt to craft a readable book. For the reader it is like being with long-time friends. Friends that do not judge you.

I try to *not* write to a specific genre. This is evidence of my generally contrary nature.

The stories in this book might be described as Fantasy or Magical-Realism or even Humor, though not all of them are funny. (fair warning!) My hope is that they will stimulate some emotions, cause a little tremor in the normality of your days.

But not too much. There is no emotional manipulation happening here.

Maybe a little.

The challenges to belief systems are minor, unless the beliefs are steeply, deeply held and irrevocably stiff. Entrenchment is heck. I seek only to entertain.

Because life is hard.

But the question is, "Hard compared to what?"

INTRODUCTION

MUCH OF WHAT FOLLOWS is derived from all the TV, Movies, Books, Comics, and Music I experienced in my life. But it also is filtered through true happenings.

The Angel thing? Truer than you might believe. The Olympian encounter? Seriously. I know those guys. The Martian thing? Let's face it, that Martian Devil girl was hot. The School Play thing? True story. Every word. Mostly.

The Sad thing? Nearly true. Don't make me talk about it.

The Avocado thing? If you've lived in Southern California, you know.

The other things? Wishful thinking in a way.

Take what you need and leave the rest.

TABLE OF CONTENTS

Angel of Reality

KEVIN WANTED A MIRACLE AND HERE IT WAS, appearing in the narthex of the cathedral: angelic, beautiful, winged, and glowing golden, a heavenly being sent down in answer to his prayer.

And then it farted.

Not some minor, low key, easy to ignore, pretend that it was some other noise in the far distance or another section of the cathedral fart, but a healthy string of bilabial fricative capped off by a significant brapping, and finishing with a piquant squee, delicate and flute-like.

The angel hovered several feet above the marble floor staring at Kevin, who remained kneeling in a posture of supplication despite his astonishment. Quiet resumed in the holy space. The fresh silence, accentuated by the previous rude noise, lengthened into tension. Finally, the angelic being again broke the silence, this time with words. "You asked for angelic help? Here I am." His voice was a strange mix of English accent and lazy drawl with a slight aroma of peppery sass.

Kevin stared in disbelief.

"I can leave," the angel said, pointing one perfect finger upwards to the heavens. The stained-glass window at the far end of the nave showed the exact same action of another angel, this one from the Middle Ages. That was the crux of the matter for Kevin; he was middle-aged and did not know how that happened. He also did not like the doctor's prognosis when he went in for his twenty-year checkup. Who knew that the middle-aged body would not tolerate the cheese puffs and carbonated, caffeine-infested sugar juices the way his once healthy, track and field, running-back body had. Now it was the Big C and a deadline, emphasis on the dead. He needed a miracle and, for the last three weeks, he prayed mightily.

"Today was a slow day," the angel said. "You were first on the list. It seems an easy enough assignment, but…" The angel bent low toward Kevin's face, "You've got to ask for what you want."

Kevin searched for the words, the most holy, most sincere, fervent, godly, humble, devout, pious words he could find. "You farted," was all that emerged from his mouth.

"Yes," the angel said, straightening back up and adjusting his robes, though they did not need adjusting. They were perfect, golden and silver, gleaming with heavenly light, just like Sunday School descriptions. "Yes, I farted. It is your fault."

Kevin was still in the thrall of disbelief. He'd been praying for a miracle but had not actually expected one. He asked for a sign from above and yet, having ignored his parentally chosen faith for most of his life, did not believe that there was any hope for such a thing to occur. He was not worthy. Or so he deeply and honestly believed. But here in front of him was the sign, the miracle, the angel waiting to grant his supplications and all Kevin had to do - all sick, cancer ridden, dying, soon to go meet his maker Kevin had to do was...ask?

The angel, eight feet tall at least, glowed from an inner light. His eyes shone with radiant beams, and sparkles dripped from his fingertips. He appeared magnificent and deific.

And he farted when he manifested and proceeded to blame the sick and dying human. For emphasis, the heavenly being let another squeaker pass. It was not without melody.

Kevin stammered, attempting to join the conversation. "Wha...why? How did I? What do you mean, I caused you to fart? Don't blame me. You are an angel! Angels don't fart!"

"Who told you that?" The peppery sass intensified. "The same person that told you we are golden and glowing? The same people that told you we have hands and feet and bodies that look like Caucasian humans? The same person that told you we have faces with eyes, ears, noses, and mouths? Does that even seem logical to you at any level?"

Once the question was poised, coupled with a rather snarky attitude for an angel, Kevin realized that it *was* a bit absurd.

"And if we have mouths, then do we not logically have throats, stomachs, intestines, and…" The angel paused and arched his left eyebrow. "…Asses?"

Kevin was losing the thrall of awe and leaning towards bewilderment. This alteration in his potential faith concerned him. He felt it might develop into actual doubt and take away the possibility of a miraculous healing. Still, how exactly was the angelic gas-passing his fault? Curiosity might kill this cat.

The angel sighed and softened his tone, though some measure of exasperation was apparent. "It is simple, really. You conjured me up by believing so hard and long and consistently." The angel sat and crossed his legs. There was nothing beneath him, but the robes draped about as if there were some great metaphysical easy chair betwixt the heavenly being's bottom and the floor of the sanctuary. "You brought me to this place by your strong faith, albeit a faith created by desperation and hopelessness. But you are as unimaginative as most others. You made me in your image, and you took the easy way. Do I look familiar to you?"

Kevin squinted and stared past the glowing light, which seemed to be fading. There he saw a handsome-looking creature with a fine jaw and strong, long nose. The cheeks were fleshy, but acceptably so, and the angel's hair was receding, giving him, to Kevin's human eyes, a wise look. The neck was a little wattle-ish, but acceptably so. Overall, a fine-looking being, still virile despite some age, and somewhat familiar...no, quite familiar, but he couldn't exactly recall where he had seen that face. Suddenly he felt his mouth gape open in shock. The angel looked just like he did! Well, except for the glowing, radiant, beaming light. Kevin blinked and looked again. The angel opened his own mouth in a mocking exaggeration and leaned close to the human.

The angel leaned back, waggling his fingers in the air and said, "And what, pray tell, did you eat last night?"

All day the taste of the previous evening's chili dog dinner remained evident in Kevin's mouth. Despite the repetitive tooth brushing and mouthwash rinsing, or the attempts to cleanse his palate with colas and energy drinks, the occasional urp of indigestion brought all his dietary sins back to the present moment. The angel brought his hand to his lips and let go an audible belch.

"I need to be healed," Kevin blurted out.

The angel, distracted by some internal gas or fluid exchange, consciously returned his attention to the human. "What?"

"I have C...canc..." Kevin found it hard to say the word. "I have a disease, and it is going to kill me. Soon. I don't want to die. I'm too young. I have things I want to do! I haven't accomplished anything in my life yet!"

"What were you waiting for?" the angel asked. The snark was still present, but the tone was softer.

"I thought I'd have time when I got older. But now I'm not getting any older. I've only got a few months to live!"

"And you're going to waste it on your knees? Doesn't seem like a good use of time remaining to me."

Kevin stood up and balled his fists. Leaning towards the angel, he shouted, "I didn't ask you here to berate me! I asked for a healing sign from heaven. Are you just going to scold me?"

The angel set a foot back on the ground. Pressing against non-corporeal armrests he hoisted himself to an upright position and swiftly extended his other leg, placing his foot right into

Kevin's crotch. Kevin returned to his knees, wheezing.

"A little respect, please," the angel said. "Transferring to and from the earth is not easy these days. No one believes the way they used to. Disbelief limits us. Too much skepticism. Everyone wants to believe, but they also don't want to look like fools. No one asks for big things anymore. They ask us for parking spaces near the grocery store door mostly. What do they think? That we are some kind of concierge service?" The angel squatted in front of Kevin, letting out a low vibrato from his nether region. Kevin, gasping for breath, did not take full notice.

"Alright, human. You have petitioned the Lord with prayer, and I am the one who answered. Here's the deal. No more junk food. No more cheap beer just to get drunk fast. Eat better. Drink pure water. Get some exercise, for God's sake, and do something constructive with your life. Quit that stupid job and work for something you believe in. I'm assuming you do not believe in convenience store clerking?" Kevin moaned an affirmative sound. The angel continued, "I'll give you two more years and, if you get it together, we will re-examine the future then. In the meantime, no doctors, no treatments. Just take responsibility for your physical self. Deal?"

Kevin rolled over on his side as the pain receded. He managed to get one eye to stay open.

"Sounds like hell. Are you sure you are not the devil?"

"We are all the same. The perception of the human makes things heavenly or hellish. Deal?"

Kevin rolled over on his back, his breath returning to some semblance of normalcy. He opened the other eye. The angel still squatted above him. "I live if I agree to live like you say? No pain? No dying? No symptoms?"

"That is the deal. No hidden clauses. No sneaky backdoor twists. I don't work that way. Too complicated. Too much to remember. Two years. Live a good, balanced life, then I check in. If you screw up…" His voice dropped and turned serious in tone, "I have a friend who looks like the grim reaper."

"Really?" Kevin asked, his eyes wide with premature fear.

The angel curled his lip in a derisive sneer. "He looks like that because that is how you will perceive him. Really, he is just in charge of transfer protocol. Still…ooooooh! SCARY!!!" The angel held his arms outstretched and waved his hands about. The room grew dark, and the sound of thunder in the distance echoed in the cathedral. Or maybe that was another basso-profundo flatus release.

Light returned, and the angel straightened up once again, brushing at his robes. "Any questions?" he asked.

Kevin pondered for a moment. It might be tough to get a handle on things and change his life, but the other option was not very appealing. "I'll do my best," he said.

"That is all we ever ask."

"One thing: if I made you in my image, and that is why you are…flatulent, how come there is no odor?"

"You're upwind," the angel said, and flapping his wings vanished into the high, arching ceiling of the cathedral. One final staccato burst sounded like the thunder of judgment, followed by a long mournful toot, as if somewhere a horn blew. The breeze from the wings ruffled Kevin's balding pate.

The scent was heavenly.

The God of Feet

IN ALL FAIRNESS, IT WAS A VERY NON-SPECIFIC PLEA that we sent heavenward. Random interpretation by any deity-like beings we didn't actually believe in was to be expected. Except we did not really expect any answer at all.

There were no obvious wings, so it can be forgiven that we did not immediately realize we had a god-like personage in front of our stalled vehicle. The gleaming golden robe, more of a tunic really, and rather short at that, and the vague emanation of light from his rail-thin form made us wonder a bit at first, but we just locked the doors and sat closer. It was the half-dome effect on the rainfall, like an invisible umbrella over his entire body, that finally drew our attention to the fact that something supernatural was occurring.

Lacey saw him first, as usual. I was too busy trying to recall anything that my intensely mechanical and practical late father might have said about engines and stalling and how to get cars moving in torrential floods. I was failing miserably, and the creek was rising. All I could come up with were poetic descriptions of the deadly, watery world around me. In the back of my mind, I was always looking for details to add to my novel. Heck, I was just looking for a way to break my writer's block. Even in the face of death.

Already, great streams of water fed downward from the mountain roadway ahead of the old car into the valley below. The old wooden bridge we were stalled upon was siphoning some of the rainwater across and away from the engorged creek, sending it cascading down the two-lane dirt road towards the old wooden town we'd recently passed through.

Olympus was the name of that antique town. It was quite an overstatement for an underachieving little burg. Not even at the peak of the mountain, it barely existed on a few dirt and gravel lanes branching off the main road, which itself was really only a county road cut through the deep forest heading up the side of this inauspicious mountain.

Olympus consisted of some not quite log houses, a general store with a new looking antique post office logo in the window, an empty shop with a sign shaped like a golden apple that said "Beauty" above the door, and a cobbler shop, which seemed a puzzling choice for occupation in such a limited population center. Then there was Festus's Service Station, which I swear had an old anvil and forge out back under a spreading chestnut tree where a village smithy might stand. We parked beneath an ancient metal carport and slept in the car the night before.

The little collection of buildings was desolate, but not a ruin. Not quite a ghost town, but not far from the title. It did show signs of recent habitation, just no habitants. "Perfect place for a murder," Lacey stated. In retrospect I realized she was looking at me when she said it.

Lacey and I expressed concern at our inability to figure out how to get even a couple gallons of gas from the unlocked station with the old-style pumps, the kind with the flying unicorn thing as a symbol.

In the garage area there were two cans filled with some gasoline-smelling fluid within. We were pretty low and the old map hanging on the wall didn't offer much hope of a next town saving grace.

The map itself looked more like an ancient scroll and was undetailed, to be charitable. We saw the town of Litochoro where we had started our scenic ascent and scattered about were symbols that might have been trees and lines that might have meant roads. Some wag even scrawled, "Here be dragons" off to the far western edge in what looked like charcoal.

A line that could be the road we were traveling from Litochoro up to the little desolate village marked it as Olympus. The surrounding names were Ptera, Vrontou, and Dion. The line from Olympus did not connect to any of them. It did indicate a town (we assumed town because the mark on the map was bigger than the others) called Ithaca. The line from where we were to that goal did not seem very direct and in fact seemed to be smudged at various places, almost erased.

The might-be gas and the apparently small distance to Ithaca seemed worth the risk, I believed, and Lacey agreed. Especially with the main road running fast with flood water.

Up the mountain seemed the better choice than down into a possibly flooding valley. I figured if we could crest the peak, gravity would let us coast down the other side even if the tank were empty.

The old Mercury had an AM radio that picked up virtually nothing while we were winding our way along the scenic backroads of America. No Bluetooth. No Sirius XM.

As honeymoons went, this one was testing the marriage vows early. Periodically I found it necessary to create new vows, the most current being that if we made it through the storm and over the mountains, returning back to civilization, I promised Lacey that the car would be auctioned as an antique and we would live in the densest city of her choosing, using only public transportation. No more backwoods adventures for us. Urban living was our future. I would learn to write my books in the midst of noisy taxi and bus traffic.

Several miles out of Olympus the gas in the containers betrayed us. The old engine was powerful enough, and in its day quite forgiving of bad gas. Twentieth Century meets Twenty-First Century unknown, unfiltered, flammable liquid.

"Maybe it was kerosene," Lacey said. "Not gasoline. They smell alike, don't they?"

"I don't know. I have never had the opportunity to do a comparison test." My tone was snarky and exasperated, but she didn't seem to notice. Hers matched mine when, with a jolt and a chug, the engine coughed and spit dark smoke out of the tailpipe and slowed to a halt. I really did not apply the brakes at all, hoping we would glide across the old wooden bridge and achieve a dubious feeling of safety on the far side.

We did not. Twenty feet from either end, smack dab in the middle, we heard a noise like "CHUNK" come from the engine compartment. The old car stopped with a lurch. Forward motion negated, we also did not roll backwards off the flat bridge. The water from the rising creek below lapped over the edge of the bridge. The opposite of safety. Not dubious at all.

"Great," Lacey muttered. "My next honeymoon will be in Cancun, I swear." I started to point out that you only get one honeymoon per marriage. Then I realized the implications. We'd been lost for two days, and I really did not believe that, in the technologically advanced Twenty-First Century, getting lost was even possible until it was happening.

Lacey had taken to muttering longer sentences as the storm clouds gathered throughout the morning. I caught a few phrases over the sound of the old engine. Things like "leave his dead body" and "push this heap over the edge of a cliff" and "start a new life," coupled with "after an appropriate period of mourning," all adding to the already tense trip.

"We have a problem," I said.

"Ya think, adventure boy? Gonna write this into your book?" The roar of the river made it difficult to hear her, but the tone of her voice was definitely not one of humor or teasing.

"We need a solution, not snark." I took the high road, as it were, quoting my insufferably optimistic editor. She would typically ask, "What would your Protagonist do?" So, I tried to think like a hero. "The car isn't likely to go forward," I mused, "and even if we push it, we are probably not strong enough to get it to go up the incline ahead."

"So, we go backward?" Lacey sounded dubiously hopeful.

The rain, of course, intensified just then. I looked at her, and in my best contrite tone said, "I know this whole trip is pretty harebrained and my stupid idea. I wanted to show you beautiful things and places in the country and relive the good old days in my dad's old car. In my mind it was to be romantic, like living in simpler times. I believed this would change your mind about living in the city. I am a fool, and I love you, and we are in trouble. Please forgive me and I am not going to beg because we don't have time for such drama, and I definitely do not want to drown in this old tank."

Logical Lacey said, "Okay. We push it backward. I will sit in the dry, driver's seat once we get it moving and hit the brakes after we are off the bridge. We can coast backward a little bit away from the river's edge and probably ride out the storm in the car, right? A second night sleeping in the back seat won't be so bad. Only tonight you sleep up front." It was not a question.

"Right," I said with a weak smile. At that moment the bridge lurched, and the back of the car swung about a foot to the left, the direction of the movement of the flood waters. Turning to look out the wide back window we saw that there was a brand-new Twenty-First Century gap between the road behind us and the bridge on which we were now trapped.

"New plan. Grab your knapsack and jacket, and we get out and run for the other side. Up the mountain on foot." A massive crash of thunder and a huge blinding flash signaled lightning striking very near. Splinters from an exploding tree scattered all around the road in front of us, and the vibration shook the car.

Lacey began screaming, "Dear god! I don't want to die. Any god! Any deity in any heaven, or in Hel...help, Help, HELP!!!" She was quite convincing in her panicked supplication, especially as she previously embraced atheism and reason as her guides to life.

And that was when we saw the angel/god/deity being/person. It was the weird golden glow that brought him to our visual attention. A bright spot in a grim, dark and stormy day. He was skinny, but muscular, like a runner in the park. And he was floating in the air.

As the encounter proceeded, I eventually observed that he had wings extending from his ankles. Not from his shoes, but the guy's actual ankles. Little white wings, not big at all. At that point of initial contact though, details were hazy. Through sheets of water cascading down the wide, front windshield I saw him beckon us to get out of the car and follow him.

Confronted with an actual, visible, potential answer to her prayer, Lacey slid over on the big bench of the front seat and clung to me, her slender hands death-clutching my favorite t-shirt and wrinkling it permanently. I thought to make a fuss. It was an original from a Franz Ferdinand concert, but then, we were on the verge of drowning, and I wasn't so concerned about the shape my clothing would be in when our bodies were found down river. One must keep their priorities in order.

The deity-being guy waved at us again and floated toward the car. The half-dome umbrella effect soon covered the driver's side door, and the sound of the pounding rain ceased to be so loud just above my head. I pressed the button to roll the window down, but just a crack. It occurred to me obliquely that the car had no power at the moment and the motion of the window must be by divine energies. Or something.

"Nice ride," he said. "These old boats were the best vehicles ever made. 1954, right?"

"Um, 57 actually." I felt the need to be accurate.

"Merc? Monterey, right? Kinda hard to tell in the rain."

"UH, Montclair I think. Granpa called it a Turnpike Cruiser. He bought it new." I could sense Lacey staring hard at us as we casually discussed the nature and lineage of the vehicle.

To forestall any emotional eruption, I sought to turn the attention back to the deity. "So…you are GOD or representative of such or merely a god-ish type being, not omnipotent as such?" I sensed that my attempt to distract Lacey had not worked and felt her winding up.

Before she could interject, and I could feel her winding up to do so, the odd fellow with the wings and invisible umbrella said with a bit of snark, "You know that the bridge is going to collapse, right? That you should abandon ship?" He chuckled. "Old boat. Abandon ship. Good one. I love a good pun."

"Who *are* you?" I asked, rolling the window all the way down. Again, I wondered about the power windows, when nothing else seemed to be working.

He did not look dangerous. In fact, I felt kind of warm and calm in his presence. The bridge shifted some more, and the calm warm fuzzy went away.

Lacey screamed again.

He seemed to notice her for the first time. "Hello there!" He leaned into the open window just a bit. "You're the one that called for help. A very fine plea. It felt quite…worthy of attention. You must be a *special* person to get through to the divine realms so easily. Come on then," he beckoned, extending his hand towards the front of the bridge. "You asked for help. Here I am."

Lacey found her voice. "Are you an angel?" She did like being called special.

The gleaming man had started to turn away, but he swung back and with a half-smile said, "Not exactly, but if you want to think of me that way go ahead. Now let's go."

"Wait," Lacey said. "I'm not going anywhere with a strange...um, stranger in the middle of some dark stormy forest. I have seen that movie."

He squinted at her, and his eyes glowed just a bit. I glanced at Lacey and saw her eyes widen and maybe glaze over a little. "Oh," he said. "You have seen a lot of those movies. Why do humans do that to themselves? Isn't life scary enough without watching those stupid Freddy and Michael type films?

"Well, to each their own, I guess. Have you seen the one where the young couple gets trapped in their classic black with red and white interior multi-ton old car as the bridge collapses into the flooded river and they are swept away to drown slowly without hope of a rescue? Terrifying." He arched both eyebrows and pressed his lips together. "Personally, I prefer the one where the young couple calls for divine aid and when it arrives, they show a little faith and get out of their doomed vehicle and accept gratefully the divine assistance of one of the old gods. Maybe even spare some devotion?"

"What old god?" Lacey asked as she straightened up and released my shirt. I knew she was having steampunk visions of Cthulhu dreaming in death in old R'lyeh, or whatever she was always on about. Personally, I never got the Lovecraft horror thing. Nothing much ever seemed to happen. Just people slowly going mad due to some unnamed creeping dread. This rain pounding on the car roof, now that would drive anyone insane. I was moderately glad that it was only on the passenger side, thanks to the weird, divine umbrella thing.

Water, previously merely lapping the edge of one side of the bridge, now was rushing over the width of the span. I watched the rising creek turning into a torrential river pouring over the old, and if the god was to be believed, doomed bridge out my window. I looked down at the fellow's feet. Where he stood was dry, and the gushing river split around him in a circle. It was like he stood in one of those upside-down jars things that people used to hang old watches and stuff inside.

"Maybe we should get going, honey." I started to reach around to grab our knapsacks. Everything we needed was inside them. We traveled fairly light and kept all the clothes in tight rolls just like the video on You Tube showed us. Every night we had to iron something. In the trunk lay extra clothes and stuff we bought on the trip. Survival would dictate that souvenir T-shirts and trinkets get sacrificed to the river gods.

Lacey's atheism raised its skeptical head once again, the demi-god's compliment spell fading completely with the thought of getting drenched. "I am not going anywhere with some self-proclaimed maybe-angel. My mother and father went that way for a while and ended up standing on street corners handing out tracts and pamphlets. I had to stand in the cold while they tried to tell everyone they met that the world was ending ten years ago. No. I want some information and facts before I follow any religious guy."

I looked down at the wings on his feet. He raised his arms, and there on his wrists were matching wings, little, white-feathered things. They fluttered a bit, then faster, and suddenly he was floating upwards. He flew, slowly, and actually, it was more like he was standing in the middle of the air, traveling a half circle over and around the heavy hood of the old Mercury, descending at Lacey's side. He knocked on the window.

"I think you should open it," I said.

"Um, yeah," Lacey replied, her disbelief dissipating. Atheism notwithstanding, winged beings hovering about offering miracles of salvation from certain fatal acts is helpful in the creation of faith.

She slid across the bench seat, reaching out to roll down the wide window. Before she got there, he waggled a finger, and the stem for the door lock popped upwards. She squeaked, not really a scream, and slid back across the long bench seat, slamming into me fast. The passenger door opened, and no rain came inside. Only the man with little wings. The invisible umbrella stretched across the top of the car, and the sound of the pounding rain lessened considerably.

The deity-being sat down with us on the big front seat. "Plenty of room," he said, running his hands across the vinyl. His hand came suspiciously close to Lacey's bare leg, but then it was close quarters for three. She did not recoil. I figured not to cause a fuss.

Closing the door, he said, "That's better. Even with the divine shielding, the sound of that rain is relentless. Maddening, if I do say. By the way, *you* called me an angel, so...not 'self-proclaimed,' right? So first..." he patted Lacey's leg, above the knee but below the hem of her shorts. "Don't worry. It is not your mother's end of the world, just a bad storm and a stalled car. Second, I have placed a couple of golden bindings, like mystical laces, on the bridge that will secure it to the earth for a few more minutes, but I am not so powerful as to alter the eventuality of the bridge being swept away, so...no, not omnipotent. Third, I don't mind the questioning so much, but we are dealing with a time constraint here, and you really should be saying 'thank you' and getting thee hence to safety and such. So, three points from me, three questions from you, but nothing too deeply philosophical and, even if you do not like the answers, no asking for more questions."

"Like wishes," I said.

"What?" he said.

"You know, like asking a genie for more wishes? You can't wish for more wishes?"

Lacey and the deity looked at me funny. "That makes no sense, asking questions for more questions? Makes no sense," Lacey said, looking at the deity.

Shrugging narrow shoulders, winged hands turned palm up, he shook his head in negative agreement. Then he arched a brow. His face was thin, and he had prominent cheekbones. Dark skin gave him a Mediterranean look, I thought, even though I had never been to the Mediterranean. His hair was wispy and white and started far back on his head. I hadn't noticed it before, but he did look a bit old.

"So, are you the supreme god or just a minor god?" Lacey asked, the snark back in her voice.

"I am the God of Feet."

"That is stupid."

"No, just the old way of believing coming back around again. Once humanity believed in many little gods, the god of trees and flowers and such, and as time went on it got a little too specific. There was a cult for a while that believed in the god of the little toe, then they splintered, and some followed a god of the little toenail. It was all me, of course. No one needs to get that specialized in their trade. The goddess of the torso has a big job, and the god of the head is pretty specific in his own way, but really, he has all the eyes and nostrils and eardrums as well as the cervical bones and brain stem, not to mention the hair follicles. That, by the way, is the least of his concerns these days, and I recommend you do not invest in any hair growth schemes."

I looked in the rearview mirror and glanced at my prematurely thinning hair. Not too bad and really, the foot god did not have much room to be talking, with a shiny, balding pate of his own.

"The God of Feet." Lacey lost some of the concern she displayed at his magical entry to the big car and now sat up straight. Her hips stayed tight to mine, however, and there was a healthy hand span between her and the old god, who was gazing intently at her sandal-clad feet and smiling weirdly.

"So, we are about to drown in a raging mountain flood and when, in panicky and irrational desperation I call out for help, the Supreme Being sends the God of Feet? Isn't that a bit pedestrian?"

"Nope. No one sent me. I just happened to be the only one available to take the call. Really, my job is pretty easy these days. Lots of shoes available, and they are all *finally* pretty good and comfortable. That memory foam is amazing! I have some on myself." He stretched his legs and pointed to the winged feet. They were clad in a kind of faux faded canvas, grayish in the dim, stormy light. I could not tell if they were comfortable, but they did look easy to slip on and off. His lean, but well-muscled legs were covered in white curly hair and, as he shifted, the tunic opened at the neck, exposing a fairly hirsute chest.

"My priestesses are making good headway, if you'll forgive the mixed allegory, and pedicure temples are expanding exponentially. Road shoe sacrifices are down, and the hanging of old gym shoes is not as popular as once before, but lost baby shoes are at an accelerated rate since the advent of cheaper baby shoes at the dollar stores. Mothers don't pay that close attention anymore, and dads? Well, they are mostly clueless about what their kid is doing in the stroller. I mean, why does a baby need a shoe anyway? Decoration, that is about it. By the way, I am always looking for new priestesses and devotees. The turnover is immense these days."

"How do you propose rescuing us, anyway?"

"Well, we walk. That is what I do these days: walking, running, jogging, some marathon action. They are all about the same except for the necessary lung capacity. Thank the torso goddess you two are in pretty good shape that way."

I was not sure, but he might have glanced at Lacey's chest just then. "I will keep you dry for a few miles, and it will be uphill, but you are young and healthy." Again, the glance. "You have never been exactly devoted to the gods. So, rescue, yes, but comfort is not promised. By the way, that whole supreme deity thing? Not as permanent a position as one might believe. Lots of burnout at the top."

"So, last question..."

"Nope, that was the last question. I just ignored the one about being pedestrian. Like I have never heard that one before. If you want to pun around me, at least be respectful. You seem to be a bit blasphemous by nature, and I can forgive that to a certain degree, but using the holy words in an attempt to mock my powers...well, I am still going to save you, but now you will be wet when it is all done. Ready?" He gripped the big chrome door handle.

Lacey reached out and laid a hand on his left arm. "Wait. This is all a weird moment, and I am sorry if I offended you, but I have never heard of the god or goddess of body parts theory of theology. Is there, like, a god of cars? A goddess of clothing? I guess I recall the Romans or someone having household gods and such, but this is the Twenty-First Century, and practically no one I know of believes in a compartmentalized heavenly realm, let alone having actual faith in a big, head god that is in charge of all-seeing everything. I really did not expect any answer to my plea. It was just sort of impulse…reactionary."

"Do you want me to go away?" he asked. "I will, but I'd rather not. I have been pretty idle for quite a few centuries. Bored really, just wandering the earth. The whole car craze of the fifties and sixties coupled with the jet set trendy stuff really took away the energy for exploration by walking. Even museums are emptier now that the internet has all the paintings and sculptures in one place. People used to cross entire continents on foot. Ah, those were the days. Always praying for relief from aching feet."

He grew quiet for a couple of heartbeats and then said brightly, "Of course there were always the mailmen and the delivery guys. Great bunch a' worshippers. That was it until the 1970s when the jogging craze started up, but even that was more about inspiring designers and answering fairly mundane prayers for a blessing of Air Jordies to be supplied to a poor kid somewhere."

He turned to face us and took Lacey's hand in his, patting it in a less than avuncular manner. "Look, you folks are my chance to perform a real miracle. Validate my existence and regain a bit of respect. You know, I save your lives, and then you will be grateful and proselytize in my name and maybe I get a following so I can show the Supreme Goddess currently in charge that I am worthy of that raise in rank I've been supplicating for. Maybe I can get some real wings, the big kind that I can wear on my back. Whatta ya say?"

I had been watching the storm out the front window as best I could. No engine, no power. No power, no wipers, and it was a lot like being in a submarine, or so I would believe, because I had never actually been in a submarine.

My side window was still down, but the divine shielding umbrella power covered the entire driver's side door. I could see mud from the rain-soaked mountain ahead really flowing now, like lava in old dinosaur movies. It was splashing upward in ever rising parabolic arcs, and I was sad for my grandad's car. It was his first, and he kept restoring the thing all his life until my father took over. It was not too special to anyone else, a little uncommon, not really rare, but it was his. A pretty thing really, shiny black with lots of chrome and the bright red and white interior made the contraption a real show piece. I believed that my brothers and I were probably conceived in the big bed of a backseat. Dad loved the car, mom loved dad.

But it was a problematic possession for anyone else. Big and gas hoggish and needing special attention all the time. It was the one thing in his will that no one else in the family wanted, and we could not get a buyer for the price my older brothers thought it was worth. Now it would get washed away, and they would posthumously blame me.

Lacey and the foot god were looking at me. "What did you say?" they asked in unison. I must have been muttering. Dad used to mutter. Maybe it was inherent to mutter inside the old Mercury.

"No way we can save the car, I guess."

"It is a nice one," the foot god replied. "A real shame to lose a beauty like this. What a way to travel. Look at this leg room!" He stretched his legs again, waving his arms about in the cavernous front seat area.

"Do you want it?" Lacey said. "Like, as a tribute? A sacrifice? Fatted calf or something? Gratitude for saving us?"

I knew she wanted to get rid of the beast, as she called it, but I would have liked to be consulted in its disposition. After all, I might not be here if it weren't for the backseat.

Lacey added slyly, "It *runs* good."

The foot god's face lit up. "Well, it would be a better way to travel around the earth: faster, more efficient, just the way the efficiency goddess likes things nowadays." He went silent, pondering.

Lacey got excited and turned toward him. "You save us. We tell everyone about the God of Feet and become your devotees. You get the miracle credit, and the car. We will live in the city and walk everywhere. Unless, of course, it is cold. Or wet. Or too hot or…"

He also got excited and, turning to face her, took both her hands in his. "Yes. Yes. Reasonable exceptions, of course. Would you consider opening up a shoe store? Well, maybe not, you have your career already, but let's keep that thought up front, alright? Just a suggestion?" Lacey and I nodded affirmatively. She more vigorously than I. There seemed to be a glow to her eyes.

"So, if we are going to worship you, what do we call you?"

"Hmmmm. I haven't had a real godly kind of name in some centuries. Nike, once." He looked at his feet, and the wings wiggled. "Maybe that was mom...so long ago...hard to remember who I was back then."

"Nike," I said. "That has soul."

He laughed. "I get that! Soul. Sole. You are funny. I get a *kick* out of puns." I laughed too. Lacey just raised her left eyebrow at the two of us. The car lurched as the bridge began its possible final collapse.

The foot god, who maybe was Nike (but I had my doubts because I had seen that statue, and it was definitely a different gender), patted his naked knees with his hands and said, "Right. Well, before we were gonna hoof it off the bridge and up the hill a ways. Now we have to get the car off as well."

He reached past Lacey and touched my arm. It was just a tap, not a grip, not a pull, but there was a period of time, it must have been just a second or two, but so much happened, and I have no clear memory. Golden light, warm breeze, unreal music that sounded like the color blue, cats that smiled, and dogs that knew the secret to the universe but when I asked them, they just wagged their tails. "Good dog," they said, and begged me to take them for a walk. Only I had the collar and leash attached to my neck. Then I found myself in the passenger seat. Lacey was now hip to hip with the foot god, who was sitting in the driver's seat. She did not move away.

"That's better," he said, running his hands around the wide steering wheel. Looking upward and out the driver's side window, he shouted, "Hey, Festus! A little help?" A large man-like being appeared in a bright flash in front of the car, not unlike the manifestation of the foot god, but more light. Once-upon-a-time-maybe-Nike waved a greeting. The big guy wore a similar tunic, but on him it looked more like a coverall. He spread his fingers and laid his palms upon the hood of the car.

"Watch this," Nike-son said, pointing to the gas gauge, which went from near empty to full in a few seconds. "I love when he does stuff like that. He can fix anything." The engine roared to life, and Festus gave a thumbs up and walked from the front to the passenger side window. It rolled down of its own accord.

Festus looked at me and said, "Ya shou'n't a called Pegasus a unicorn. That's why the gas didn't work."

Probably-not-Nike said, "Hey bro', what's shakin'?"

"Long time, pal," Festus said. I wondered at the weird non-heavenly sounding slangy lingo these two were communicating in.

"Lacey, meet my brother Festus, once a master smithy, nowadays the god of combustion. Festus, this is Lacey and her, um, husband." Apparently, I did not rate a name, and I wondered at the way he knew hers. I wondered too why I was getting the rap for the unicorn remark. I was pretty certain that was Lacey. Still, torrential rain, crumbling bridge gods from the past. Some things a person can let slide.

"You gotta get going, Herm," Festus said with genuine concern in his voice, authoritatively naming our new deity while looking at the bridge behind us. Terrible tearing noises were occurring, and the shuddering rocked the heavy Mercury on its mighty springs. "Time to *forge* ahead," Festus said, and the god now called "Herm" laughed.

"I'll get back there and give ya a sign," Festus said, walking to the end of the bridge.

The wooden structure shuddered and shifted a few more times and suddenly straightened out. I could see that we were off center from the road ahead by almost a lane and a half.

Despite being outside and some distance away, Festus's voice filled the interior of the car. "Gun it, *lead* foot!" he yelled and Herm, previously known as Maybe-Nike, shifted into reverse and stomped hard on the accelerator.

Seat belts would have been nice. I flew off the vinyl seat and slammed into the dash. As I slid to the floor, I saw Nike's son had his right arm across Lacey's chest, restraining her and copping a feel at the same time. The look of excitement on her face told me she did not mind as much as I did. The old Merc' powered backwards off the bridge, passing big Festus, who, I noted in passing, and in pain, had his name stitched on his tunic in script over his left breast. I regained the seat, struggling against the gravitic and velocity forces of the burst of reverse motion. Watching through the front windshield I saw the bridge slide away from the road and float away down the torrential flooding river.

Just when I managed to get my back against the seat, Herm slammed on the brakes, causing the car to swerve and skid about in the running mud. I slammed against the dash again, then the door, and finally was thrown back to the floor once more. The car came to a halt. Herm and Lacey were laughing, she a bit desperately, possibly because her life was just saved in the nick of time. He threw an arm about her shoulder and pulled her close. I noticed his hair was not so white as I had thought and even looked rather dark with some distinguished gray at the temples. There was definitely more of it now.

The passenger side door opened and, because I had come to rest with my head against it, I fell out, splashing onto the muddy road. Lacey laughed again, and this time it definitely seemed like hysteria had set in. Festus, who had opened the door, reached down and grabbed me by my shirt, helping me up. He was huge in the torso but had strange skinny legs.

"Ya doin' okay?" he asked, again with genuine concern. My good T-shirt, now hopelessly pulled out of shape, was sodden and filthy. My rain-soaked jeans were getting heavier by the second. A deity was sitting in the driver's seat with my, I now suspected, soon to be ex-wife and getting ready to take possession of the title to the car. Mud was up to my ankles. "Yeah. Fine," I lied. And it occurred to me that I was lying to a god.

"Good. Well. Me an' Herm', we gotta get going. Town's down that away." Festus pointed in the direction of the empty village where we had swiped the Pegasus gas. I recalled the sign outside the gas station. "Festus's," it said, and I mentally questioned the grammar.

The big god continued, "Pretty quiet these days. You can get some good writing done there. Maybe write about us. We could use some attention. People don' believe in a god, then the god don' have no power."

"Hey! Wait a minute." I grabbed Festus by the arm, finding my courage but not my sense. His biceps were about the size of my head. "What about my car? What about my wife? What about my laptop?"

Festus looked at my small hand, soft from a lifetime of keyboarding and mouse activity. I let gravity lower it away from the god of combustion as naturally as possible. "Hermes," he said, jerking a thumb towards the driver. "He is quite a trickster, hey? You are safe now, and he gets the car, that were the deal, weren't it? The girl, well, she be tradin' up, I would guess. Yeah, this could be his big break from that demotion after the Romans and Visigoths debacle. Even if not...nice car. Not Rolls Royce, but maybe we'll get one o' their hood ornaments." He leaned forward and put his massively muscled arms out behind him like wings. I recalled that statue too. Winged Victory.

He bent low, wedging his mighty frame into the front seat. Lacey remained, pressed into Hermes, or so I guessed because I could not actually see her past Festus. The old car's restored black paint job shimmered, and the chrome gleamed like it was lit from within as Festus got inside.

The image of flames appeared on the back panels just past the wheels. It may have been an illusion, but just as the umbrella of divine rain protection finished dissipating from around the car, I thought I saw little wings form on the front and back bumpers. The car lifted up into the air.

"Have you ever been to the Greek Isles, my dear?" I heard Hermes say.

"Is Cancun one of them, Herm?" Lacey asked.

"Close enough," said Hermes as the car flew off into the downpour.

With the bridge now out of the equation, there was no more running mud being funneled down the road from the mountainside above. Plenty of muck and mire remained. Torrents of rain were diluting it and washing it away off to the sides and on down the hill, but it was still up to my ankles where I stood.

My backpack was sitting in the middle of the road in the thinning mud. Hermes must have wanted me to keep on writing, for there was a miniature version of the divine umbrella keeping it from getting soaked. My laptop would be dry. Stepping towards it I felt the thick sludge suck my slip-on shoes from my feet. Sodden socks soon followed. I stood barefoot in the middle of the road.

Weirdly enough, it felt good to have my feet squishing through the soggy earth. Cold, yes, but different than the sidewalk of the city. I felt myself stand straighter. Several thoracic vertebrae snapped and cracked like pistol shots, as if the mountain gave me a chiropractic treatment.

Picking up my backpack and slipping my arms through the loops, the miniature divine umbrella that protected the backpack now also covered my head and shoulders. I turned and watched my shoes flow down the hill in a river of sludge.

Looking towards Olympus, I thought, "Sacrifices must be made." Stepping forward, which was not as backward as I might have believed an hour before, I began to slide down the road, like a surfer, only in a mud flow. I wondered if the cobbler shop would have anything in my size.

Thinking about my laptop, I looked at the skies and said aloud, "I wonder if there is any power in town?" Thunder followed a flash of lightning. I followed the thunder.

Alternate Reality
and the School Play

PERHAPS DOORS REGULARLY LED TO ALTERNATE DIMENSIONS but today seemed particularly unfair to Katie Becker. Stepping out of one's front door should lead to the driveway and the Toyota minivan. Not a woman-eating plant.

She was less upset at the fact that a botanical aberration was seeking to devour her headfirst than that her little daughter Maddie's school play practice was not going to get the costumes Katie had so diligently worked on this last month.

A tongue-like protuberance was pressing against her head and really messing up her hair. It was not styled by any means, but she did spend extra time conditioning and brushing her shoulder-length hair to make it look at least a little special. What she really wanted was to have her hair done professionally, a rare luxury, but she was waiting to treat herself for Maddie's actual opening night. At least she had not wasted any money.

But ick! Pointy spikes were pricking her neck and throat, and it might have been worse if not for the thick turtleneck sweater she wore. The gooey syrup exuding from the interior of the flesh-eating flower was probably going to leave a stain.

Even this did not anger her. Things had a right to try and survive. The gazelle does not get angry at the lion, she thought, seeking a Zen state. It was something her yoga instructor might say.

What really bothered her was that the self-righteous Mary Jane Rasmussen would now have one more thing to fuss about. That woman was an *inveterate* bossy pants and know-it-all.

That woman!

She acted like she was the secret boss of all the parents at school. It felt like she targeted Katie from the beginning, always making "suggestions" for how something could be accomplished, or "suggesting" that Katie volunteer for a specific project. Whenever she did her "suggesting" thing Katie felt like she was back in grade school. Her, an accomplished, professional woman…well, once upon a time.

Of course, Mary Jane already put four of her eight boys through the school system, so she did know her way around, and there was some experience behind the suggestions. Katie only had Maddie. She was pretty certain that Mary Jane was more than a little jealous of her daughter.

Really? Eight boys? Eight anything? And that jock strap of a husband that never helped out and only made a spectacle of boorish behavior at any of the sporting events the boys were forced into must have been a source of constant comparison to her own Herman, who was always at the plays and practices and functions helping out - not just Maddie, but anyone who needed help. Quiet and unobtrusive, he always was the first to offer to fetch more water for Kool-Aid or open more cookies and place them in neat rows on the trays. He never drew attention to himself. Katie felt blessed with Herman.

The word *inveterate* was interesting to her just then; it made her think of the word invertebrate. It gave her an idea on how to extricate herself from this unique predicament. Katie locked her hands around the stem of the plant and, with her head still held within the giant flower, began to rock her own body back and forth, left and right. Feeling woozy, kind of euphoric, she theorized that this otherworldly creature might be attempting to inject some sort of nerve toxin into her, its prey, to calm her down and make the digestive process easier.

Well, she too had the right to try and survive, and more importantly, to get back to her own driveway and the children's costumes. The air inside the plant was thick and lacking oxygen. The tongue took up a lot of space, and then there was her own head. The walls of the thing were translucent, so she could see alright, but the goo kept making her close her eyes. She forced her hands to keep a tightening grip.

Katie was about to swoon when the stem snapped backward, seeking escape from her clutches. The flower released its gooey grip on her noggin. Falling back and away, Katie did not mean to sit down, but weariness and weirdness took hold, and her legs buckled. The ground was soft, and while not yielding, was not too hard either.

Laying back to catch her breath, she looked upward through the goo covering her face. She marveled a bit at the electric-blue cloud formations above and the weird orange lights floating in the hazy violet sky.

Briefly she pondered the possibility that she was experiencing hallucinatory images. If so, she wondered, when did they start? When she opened the door to her suburban home? The foyer looked fine. The walk to carry the costumes to the car had been normal.

Bear, cat, lobster: she took inventory as she moved from house to vehicle and recalled that every single creature was in attendance, though void its K through 6 host. The host creatures were awaiting her arrival at the school and were no doubt in last-minute practice of the animal songs and uncomplicated stage directions. Some mix of Noah's Ark and Disney movies derivation, adaptations carefully thought out so as not to violate copyright or theological belief systems.

Maddie was so excited. She was the bat. Not the superhero one. Katie was careful to impress her with that fact, but she agreed that secretly Maddie could pretend the wings were actually a cape and she was merely in disguise awaiting an arch rival. Not an enemy though. No fighting allowed. Maddie perfected her flourish of wings/cape in secret. A rival was someone who challenged you to be better, rise above your perceived limitations. An enemy...well, no seven-year-olds were allowed to have enemies.

The costumes, thirty-two varied and unique specimens created, were a job well done, even if Katie had been volunteered for it by Bossy Pants, who somehow learned that she possessed and actually knew how to operate a sewing machine. The sense of accomplishment...well, that was not there, but she was doing this for the school, for Maddie, for the class and for...she had to admit it, she was doing it because of that darned Mary Jane Rasmussen.

That would be Ras-MUS-sen, not RAS-muss-en, like Katie first pronounced it. She was instantly corrected in front of everyone at the school booster meeting and co-op. The correcting never seemed to end with Mary Jane.

For Maddie, Katie endured it all and even looked forward to some of the upcoming events. But it was not what she would call satisfying. Life, *her life*, was supposed to be different. The marriage was supposed to be more…equal? No, that was not the correct word exactly. More *together* perhaps. She and Herman were to travel together on his business trips. She would handle packing and paperwork for him, and he would buy and sell imported goods and exotic products. But young and in love often brings on children. So it was, and they agreed. He businessed. She mommed.

Agreed. It seemed it was all she did these days, agreed with others as to what would be done for the school, for the children, for Maddie. But what about for Katie? Well, there was Maddie, and that was a big plus.

Katie still caught herself wishing that she might one day be able to slip away from her tasks and explore the world. Once she was an adventurous little tomboy. Now she was dutiful and a fine little housewife. It was the twenty-first century, for goodness' sake, and she was living like a Stepford wife.

****

When everything had been inventoried, packed, and in the vehicle, Katie thought about the jungle scenery awaiting the little creatures in their makeshift animal costumes. This chaos was temporary. The children seemed to be enjoying the process, but for Katie, an introvert by nature and always being expected to apologize for her personal normal, the rampant activity gave her a sense of being mentally violated.

The sewing machine assignment was really a bit of a blessing. Quiet and focused, she was contributing, but not quite in the thick of things. Only the dress rehearsal was an expectation. This Wednesday night and then the two main performances, Friday and Saturday. If they sold enough tickets, there might be a special Sunday Matinee. She needed be there with needle and thread for last-minute tailoring and the inevitable repairs.

Katie had let her eyes scan the hallway and their not-so-formal dining area which was doing temporary duty as the makeshift sewing room. The "Animal Factory" Herman called it.

Walking to the door, reaching for the handle, desperately desiring a shift, a change, some form of rescue and feeling guilty about the selfish desire she was experiencing, she said aloud, "I need a different jungle." Looking at the little good luck statue Herman received from one of his clients in

Hong Kong, she added, "I need a quiet jungle to relax in." The door opened and…

****

Using her forefinger only, for she was illogically hoping to keep her hands relatively clean, she wiped the goo away from her eyes first, then off her forehead, and finally from her cheeks. Eventually she gave in and used her entire hand, wiping the stuff off and away from her hair the best she could. Curly red became slick, straight russet. She snapped her wrists, and goo flew off onto the surrounding fauna.

Fairly normal looking trees, for the most part, though the colors were quite brilliant, and the leaves iridescent. One shivered, and branches slid across vines and made gentle musical noise. She kept her distance. The woman-eating plant stem thrashed about a while, and it looked like the flower was coughing. She did not know if she killed the poor thing, but it wasn't happy. Katie watched in respectful silence, wishing that if there were a consciousness attached, it would reincarnate in a less predatory and more evolved fashion.

Then the big flies arrived. Clouds of them, and they all wanted to sup the goo that remained around her face and neck. She rose and ran. But they were fast. Not really flies at all, she saw as they swarmed her head, but almost like tiny little monkeys with wings. Not the *Wizard of Oz* wicked witch kind, not so scary looking. They had long appendages that trailed out behind them like tails and smaller arm-like things with little hand-like grabby things, three-fingered, and they were all opposable to one another, so grasping and carrying was easy. The wings were truly insect-style and yet not wide like one might expect in a creature this size.

She recalled the old tale about bumble bee wings not being aerodynamic enough to carry the bee, making it scientifically impossible for them to fly. They were proof of a miracle, or so the motivational speaker said. Herman said that story had been disproven, but he could not explain why. She chose to believe the miracle aspect rather than lose the magic of bumble bee flight. She liked the idea of magic in the universe. Especially while she was home alone doing chores.

Little statues and fetishes littered the shelves, and odd pictures of strange semi-deities were scattered about the walls and halls of their large-ish, older fixer-upper. They mostly blended into the background of her life, but she always rubbed the belly of the weird little monkey-cat thing that Herman brought back from one of his business trips. Perhaps India? She could not recall just then, but she did remember rubbing the brass belly right before leaving for the school. Just for luck, she thought, but then, she had thought again and said out loud, "I hope today is not too boring. I am tired of being bored."

Just then, the clock chimed the hour, a signal that she was running late. "I wish," she had said, "that I had time to relax just a bit." Bolting for the door she watched it swing open, and she saw the weird world. Too fast she moved forward and too slow she backpedaled. Her first steps past the door jamb were on a not too tall, but steep, hill. She was proud that she did not tumble, only stumble. Katie did stagger, not quite in control of her body. The woman-eating plant was waiting at the bottom. Katie heard her front door close. All this came back to her as she scurried, seeking succor from the flying pests.

The monkey flies were cute enough that she did not want to swat them and squish their little faces. They did cling as she ran - but seemed respectful of her eyes, ears, and nose. She did not need to open her mouth to breathe. Runner's lungs. She ran out of the jungle, making certain to remain out of reach of tree branches and suspicious shrubbery. The world opened up into a large field of odd, tall, grass-like foliage.

The grassy stuff, yellow stalks with orange heads, like wheat in a way, but different, grew tall and then short and then tall, creating a neat wave pattern. As she ran it split apart, creating a Katie-wide path. She felt the sense of consciousness, that it was letting her pass. The ground below, which possessed a faint blue glow, was visible through the neatly ordered stalks.

The monkey flies did not bother her so much in the taller areas, the stuff that grew above her head, but they gathered when she was amongst the shorter stalks. She came to a spot where there was a wall of red and green striped rocks, rising vertically. The flying monkeys swarmed again.

Off to her left, away from the barrier of stone, the grassy wheat-like stuff continued parting. She took the easy path and dashed that way. Here all the grass grew taller than her head. As she ran, she noted the flying monkey flies were lessening in number.

Little whip snaps were sounding around her. From her peripheral vision she watched the tips of the wheat slap things out of the air. Each snap was accompanied by a pleasant citrusy scent. As the tiny, winged monkeys fell, the glowing ground opened into little holes. The tiny fliers rolled up into little balls and settled into the dynamic depressions. Pausing, Katie watched, and it appeared that they smiled as the ground closed around them. Pleasant little mewping noises emanated from them, like kittens seeing their mother. The thought came to her that it might be best not to stop to observe, lest the holes get larger, more woman sized.

The grass path formed yards ahead of her. She did not think then to look behind to see if it was closing. She began to suspect that she was being led somewhere and considered slowing down. Before thought became decision, she arrived at a wide lake. Once again, her headlong speed made it impossible to stop, and momentum carried her several steps into the mass of fluid.

Perhaps it was a river, but there was no obvious flow nor opposite shore. Indeed, a low bank of mist limited visibility. The fluid in it was silvery and not quite clear. Sparkles were seen in the small crests of gentle waves, more like large ripples really.

The waves moved slowly, and that is why she knew it was not water. Oily motion. It was warm and not unpleasant to touch, but a little weird when one expects watery texture.

The rush into the lake splashed fluid upward, and she felt her good sweater getting soaked. The heavy wool clung to her form. She stopped and stood in the lake, realizing that none of the fly monkeys were around her any longer. They were, in fact, nowhere to be seen.

Looking back the way she came, she saw no trace of a path.

Despair descended. Katie was lost.

As these things go, she felt she had done remarkably well so far. A strange world, an unexpected arrival, coping with immediate life-threatening situations that no amount of earthly training could prepare her for, adapting to the environment, the heightened sense of danger, an increased awareness of assessment of risk – it all made her feel she could be just a little proud of herself so far. But getting lost?

Herman would be so cross. The man was a walking compass. He had star maps memorized. He could tell where he was on Earth by the scent of the air. Of course, he would be helpless here because this truly was not Earth.

She held the wet sweater away from her body and noted that the silvery fluid apparently enjoyed the sappy mess from the woman-eating flower. The flower goo was dissolving away and leaving the sweater quite clean. It also was not stretching out the way it would in real water. Despair receded. Katie slipped her favorite sweater, previously thought ruined, over her head, and there, on a strange planet, clothed only in her jeans and bra, rinsed the turtleneck out in a weird lake.

Maybe, she thought, I look a little like a barbarian warrior-goddess character. The lake cast a reflection, and she saw herself. Red hair mussed and pale white skin, freckled across chest and shoulders. And tiny. She was trim and relatively muscular. She ran and worked out.

Mary Jane Rasmussen's peer pressure was mostly the reason, but she did like to listen to books and the gym allowed her a level of guilt-free privacy. So...fit, but not barbaric. Certainly, no

Red Sonja. She was not sculpted. She was cute. She ducked her cute head into the not-lake, rinsing her face, neck, and red hair free of the plant goo. Standing up she felt remarkably clear-headed.

The not-water slid easily down her skin and also felt quite refreshing. Bracing, like an exfoliate treatment. Or a sugar scrub. Not that Katie would ever spend money on such things, but she imagined how good that might feel.

The grass on the shore shivered. Katie felt no wind. Looking up she saw five sets of eyes looking back. She squeaked, not screamed. She was proud of that. Despite the squeaking she pulled the sweater to her chest, covering herself up in latent earthling modesty.

The eyes were taller than the tall grass and attached to blue elephants. Katie was certain they were not actual elephants. It was just the impression she got, but the creatures were definitely blue. They gazed at her in silence until the big one raised its short trunk and trumpeted at her. Only it was a bit more like clarinetted at her, for the trunk was short and narrow and the sound more woodwind than brass.

Maddie wanted to play trumpet in band this year, but Katie prevailed in getting her to carry the clarinet instead. It seemed less a marching band/sporting event instrument than the trumpet and more of a jazzy Benny Goodman-style classy nostalgia sound. Of course, Miles Davis played trumpet, but Maddie was only ten, and Katie didn't want to create too much expectation or become a stage mom.

Six tentacles wrapped around her legs and waist. This time she screamed. Whatever grabbed her began to pull her deeper into the lake. The two female elephants, or so she assumed by their size, raised their own short trunks and returned Katie's vocalizing by fluting back, higher pitched than the clarinet sounds made by the male.

Despite the tentacles tugging at her, Katie's feet would not move. Something else had woven itself around her ankles. A tug of war ensued, but neither side was dominant. Katie became less scared and more annoyed. She was being jerked at the waist and almost fell in twice. Despite her initial aversion to touching the squishy, wet, sucker-laden appendages, Katie tried to peel off the tentacles and succeeded, one at a time, for they were not very strong. But she was working one handed, the other holding her good sweater. Lunging forward toward shore she broke the grip of four of the tentacles briefly, long enough to slip the sweater over her head. It was not modesty, but the reluctance to drop the cherished garment.

Trying to lift her feet from the predatory seaweed, for that is what she theorized it to be, was not impossible, but it did take sustained effort. The tentacles moved around her from back to front. She looked down saw the octopussy-looking thing. It reached upward for her neck.

"Goddamit! Enough! This is my good sweater. You can't ruin it, and you definitely cannot have it. It simply. Will. Not. Fit. You." She shouted the words, all the while punching her fist into what she imagined was the creature's face.

The two smaller blue elephants, the ones that answered her scream with the flute-like sounds, entered the lake. One of them came near her and stomped its forefoot close to her side. It did not squish the octothingy (really a sextothingy, Katie thought, for it did not have the prerequisite eight arms, only six), but the seaweed loosened its hold on her feet. The octo-sexto-pus was taking damage from Katie's fist but was reluctant to loosen its grip on her sweater.

A baby-blue colored elephant (Katie thought it might be nice if they ever had a boy to paint his room that exact tone of blue) slipped his young, thin, trunk-like appendage around the tentacled, sweater-loving life form and gave it a little squeeze.

Katie watched as the sextopus's eyes opened wider. She had the impression of surprise and maybe discomfort. Whatever. The effect of the baby not-elephant grabbing it was that it released its hold on Katie, flailing its tentacles backward, searching to grip the baby.

The little elephant made a noise, like a kazoo laughing, and tossed the squiddy being far out to the center of the lake. It was quite a prodigious throw. Katie, free from the clinging seaweed, turned and watched as the thing curled into a ball and hit the surface with a small splash.

The oily nature of the fluid did not allow for much of a splash effect. The sound was more a plop than a sploosh. Turning back, Katie saw that she was surrounded by blue. Briefly she pondered the need for fear amongst such large beasts and quickly rejected the concept. They had saved her life, sort of, even though, up to a point, she was doing okay on her own. But she appreciated the help. Have an attitude of gratitude.

"Thank you," she said. "All of you. Thanks for saving me. I am a stranger here and am…lost. Do you understand me at all?" The elephants proceeded to drink from the lake and paid her no more attention.

Lost. It was the biggest word Katie ever uttered. Standing still for the first time and not being threatened with weird death, she was able to take a quiet breath. Calm brain, calm heart. Or so her tea bag tag said this morning. Morning. That was a while ago, at least according to her internal biological timekeeper. How long had she been here? What was local time? How would she fare during whatever passed for night in this world?

The oily, silvery, not-water dried quite fast, and the only portions of her body still feeling wet were the parts still in the lake.

Okay. Step one. Step out of the pond. The journey of a thousand miles, like the journey to find her front door, began with a single step. She reached the shore, and the big male elephant wrapped his trunk around her waist, picked her up with some slight effort, and placed her back in the water. The two females placed themselves between her and the land and continued to drink.

Feeling exasperated, but also bowing to inevitability, Katie said to them, "Native wisdom? Or are you just trying to frustrate me?" They kept drinking.

They appeared pachyderm-ish, but as Katie looked closer, she saw a fine fur covering much of their bodies. They were slimmer than elephants but fairly large. The impression of elephantism faded. The baby tapped her on the back. Turning, she looked into his eyes. Human eyes. The eyes of a child, certainly. It raised its trunk and gave her a smile.

Dipping its proboscis-trunk thing into the silvery water, it sucked fluid and swallowed. It did not squirt any into its mouth. Tapping her on the chest, he repeated the process and then tapped her own small, pert nose.

"You want me to inhale the fluid? How about I just take a drink?" He shook his big head and repeated the inhalation demonstration.

"I'm sorry. I don't even know if this stuff is compatible with my biology. What if it is poisonous to humans?" Tap on the chest. Tap on the face near her nose. Repeat the sucking through his long nose.

"Okay. I am trusting you, but you have the advantage in the nasal capability section. I'm just going to take a sip through my lips." And she did, and she gagged at the taste. Choking and coughing, she doubled over and almost fell into the lake.

The baby laughed that kazoo sound again. The two females moved close and pressed against her to hold her above the surface. One pressed against her back and the other her front. Together they squeezed her just enough and with a rhythm that helped calm her cough spasms. When that subsided, they moved apart and continued to drink. Or rather inhale, apparently.

The baby looked at her and cocked his head. He actually raised one eyebrow ridge. Katie said, "See? It might be poison to me." She stopped when he tapped her mouth and pointed, using the trunk, to his own.

He stuck out his tongue and made a strange noise that put her in mind of some of the rude noises Mary Jane Rasmussen's boys made when they were at the school potluck dinners. Mary Jane never seemed embarrassed by their displays of vulgarity. Perhaps she was inured. Perhaps she just did not care. Herman never commented, and Katie wondered if she should feel embarrassed for Mary Jane. Herman never even passed gas in front of Katie. Never.

The baby elephant tapped her nose, bowed his head, and placed his face below the surface. Bubbles formed around his head and soon he raised his face back up. Tap her nose. Repeat the inhaling. Katie bowed her head and forced herself to take a nasal swig of the water. It was not so hard. Not as hard as using the Neti Pot her crabby yoga teacher forced on her when she was down with the flu last year.

In fact, the silvery fluid went in fairly easy. In a moment her head felt clear and calm, the world looked brighter, and she felt a powerful optimism about her life and everyone in it. Upbeat thoughts flooded her consciousness.

There are no obstacles, only opportunities.

Be the change you wish to see.

Every day may not be good, but there is good in every day.

Those who say it cannot be done should get out of the way of those doing it.

If you do not go after what you want, you will never get it.

If you do not step forward, you will always be in the same place.

If you always do what you've always done, you'll always get what you always got.

Whether you think you can or think you can't you are probably right.

*If life gives you lemons...*the lofty concepts began to trail off, but Katie felt clarified. "Stop being such a negative Nellie and start going with the flow!" She said it out loud, and Baby Blue kazooed triumphantly.

Mary Jane was not her foe, she understood then. Rather, she was just trying to pass on some hard-earned wisdom, some traditions that would make Katie's and other parents' lives easier. She was looked at by everyone as a bossy pants, but Katie saw clearly that Mary Jane Ras*mus*sen was in fact seeking support, attempting to form a tribe of her own, making her little corner of the world better, more efficient, and thus more pleasant, and she just wanted everyone to appreciate her efforts.

She probably never got a thank you or any validation at home. She worked so hard for everyone else and never seemed to take time for herself. What, Katie wondered, would Mary Jane actually want to do if she had a day off? A day away from her *Lord of the Flies* household?

Katie ducked her head below the not-water again and again, taking deep snorts of the fluid. The feeling of exhilaration was marvelous. Finally, the baby tapped her chest and held his nose there, preventing her from descending again. The big male (Katie could visibly confirm its maleness now as it moved away from her through the water) and the two females (same deal) were about ten yards off, and the baby gave Katie a little push in that same direction.

"Adopting me?" Katie said, smiling as she reached out to pat the creature's forehead. It seemed the right thing to do just then, and he leaned into her hand in what seemed to be pleasure. They walked a ways in the not-water, close to the shore, but parallel.

A strange vibration was growing in the air. Like thunder in a way, but as she looked around, the sky did not seem to indicate a storm formation. The not-elephants slowed down as the sound grew louder still. The male turned, staring at the shore. The two females took a stance near him, but on both his right and left sides. The baby stayed slightly behind the others and pulled at Katie's sweater to get her to join him. Hollering and hooting suddenly filled the air.

From back the way she had come, the grass shuddered, and the soil of whatever planet this was, was being thrown upward in great clods. Large anthropoid-looking beings came dashing through the field, chasing each other and leaping about with wild abandon. Dignified and serene, the blue elephants stood still, watching the unseemly behavior.

The wild troop was analogous to chimpanzees, though once again, the comparison was not entirely apt. It was only Katie's mind trying to make some sense out of the strange trip she had embarked upon. They were green, in many shades from olive drab to lime, and possibly seven-fingered, though it was difficult to count in the mad rush. Huge shocks of hair stood straight up like Mohawks on some of the larger creatures and longer locks flowed on the smaller. The smallest, the children she assumed, had hair sticking out in every direction across their heads.

Chaos and lots of it. It was a stampede, and it looked like they were having fun. The elephants in retrospect seemed to have been aware of the impending traffic. That is why they kept her from the land. After the green chimps moved past, the blue family strode up to the shore and out of the not-water. The land itself continued to quiver long after the chaos chimps moved on. The grass, far from being crushed and ground down, was beginning to loosen from the tangle and stand erect once again. It parted for the elephants as they followed in the wake of the chimpangreenzees.

Katie wondered at their direction and purpose, but the residual effects of the not-water snorting maintained within her consciousness an air of beatific zen-ness. The world, this one and the earth and whatever other planets might exist, were quite marvelous and, if not safe exactly, were still worth living on, in, and with. No matter the troubles she faced or the disappointments, she felt determination to keep a level of joy in her heart and an intense desire to never get annoyed at anyone again. Not even if they were a bossy pants. The world, she decided, needed some bossy pants people to get things done.

They walked along, and she felt companionable in the presence of the Blues. The light never waned or brightened, and day seemed to last forever. It was all timeless and perfect just the way it was. She felt no hunger and no thirst and most of all, no urgency.

She did worry about the costumes a little, but at the moment there was little she could do about that situation. Would someone wonder where she had gotten to? Would they come to the house and search for her? Would they see the costumes in the minivan and take them to the school play for use while the police filled out a missing person's report? It was out of her hands.

Trees began to appear sporadically and then frequently, and soon they were back within a more foresty type of land. Katie watched the taller, higher branches of the trees lean away from the Blues as they passed by, as if granting them an easy passage. Ahead there was chatter and noise, similar to the passing of the greens, but much quieter.

They came to a grove, and the trees there grew tall. The branches wound in loops and whorls, granting many spaces for the not-monkeys to sit, lay, and lounge, relaxing and socializing. When the Blues arrived, the cacophony rose again, and the not-elephants paused part way into the grove. A wild whistle cut through the noise of the chimpiegreenies.

"ENOUGH!" came a familiar voice. At the center of the grove was one of the woman-eating plants. Sitting beneath it, with the flower partially covering her head, was Mary Jane Rasmussen. Katie felt shock, and not a little awe.

The primates immediately went silent. Katie recognized the reaction from watching Mary Jane whistle and shout at her own troop of eight semi-chimps. "Ah! There you are, Katie. I was hoping you'd be along soon. I figured out what happened when I went past your house on the way to the school and saw the back of the minivan still open. You need to more careful in the future. Even in our town some of the kids can be mischievous. They don't mean to steal, just play tricks and such, but it's so annoying!"

Katie searched for words. She was flabbergasted. The plant appeared to be massaging Mary Jane's head. Slowly it released the woman, and a cloud of the flying monkey flies appeared and proceeded to swarm her hair. The goo was soon removed, and the style that Katie was accustomed to seeing on Mary Jane's head appeared. In a short time, she was coiffed and neat. Black bangs neat and straight across her forehead with a Betty Page curl all around the shoulder-length hair.

"Come, Katie, that slick look is so nineties. You have such beautiful hair. It should be shown to better effect." Mary Jane stood up and patted a small hillock, indicating for her to sit. Numb and still partially uncomprehending, Katie approached the flower, following the woman's instructions out of habit rather than new-found empathic alliance.

"There. I know this is strange. The first time is always a bit odd, but I am glad you found this place on your own. I always knew you were of good stuff. Capable, that is what I told them when I first saw you. That is why I became your friend right away."

Katie sat. Despite some trepidation, she allowed the not-woman-eating but rather hair-styling plant and its attendant style monkey flies to act on her hair. The giant flower closed about her, and the pointed parts began to comb through and massage her scalp. The sense of euphoria returned. This time she did not resist, did not try to escape or kill what she believed was a predator. The process felt wonderful. The bliss from the not-water was equaled or even surpassed by the experience. When the process was finished, she opened her eyes, not realizing that she had drifted off from full consciousness.

Mary Jane was eating a purple and green fruit. She handed Katie a smaller one and said, "You'll like the younger ones. More tender and sweet. I like them more ripe. Bold flavor and firmer. Like me, I guess. You are sweeter than I ever was. I admire that. I have to be too much of a bossy pants all the time or nothing gets done. I appreciate that you never give me any grief about it all. I knew right away, the first day we met, that you would understand."

One of the younger chimpy creatures was near her. Mary Jane petted his hair. It stuck straight up, and she played with it a little, parting it and slicking it back. A cowlick formed, and Mary Jane just laughed. Katie did not recall her ever laughing.

"What is this place? Mary Jane! What are you doing here? What are WE doing here? We have to get the costumes to school! The play!"

"Hush, Katie. No need to panic. You're not the type to panic. The costumes are already there. When we are done here, we will go back through our doors, and the time will be just a few minutes past when we left. It always works that way. I don't know why."

"Where are we?"

"Wonderland, maybe? I'm not really sure. Sometimes I wonder, but I have too much of a good time here to ever ask too many questions. I'm afraid it will all go away, or I won't be able to get back here. I'm not sure how I got here in the first place except that whenever the stress is too much, or the boys are too wild, or their father is too...well, too much information there.

"I just start to wish myself somewhere else. This is the place I first went to, and it is the place I choose for now. I can't get here all the time, but often. And now that you can join me, well, that just makes the world better by yards and miles. I need my best friend here to share with me."

Katie wanted to say, "You think we are best friends?" but then thought better of it and instead asked, "Are there others that come here?"

"Some, but I don't know them from the other world, the earth world. And some of them are not from Earth at all. What a variety of life forms there must be throughout the whole universe! I'm glad you fell in with the Ganeshes. They are so sweet to everyone, and they make sure we are all comfy. The little Hanumans are so helpful too." She held out a finger, and one of the flying monkey-things landed on it.

Mary Jane nodded towards the hair-grooming plant. "And I just love the Audreys. They do such a marvelous job on my hair, and I feel so balanced and relaxed after they are finished. I think they like brain waves. Especially if the brain waves are a bit scattered or flustered. The Audreys always seem so excited when I first get here, and that is usually when I am at my most mentally harassed and emotionally end-of-my-ropiness."

"Oh, Migod! Mary Jane, I attacked one when I arrived. I might have killed it!"

"No, no. It's okay. They are all connected, I think. The roots run deep, and they support one another. Like you and I do at the school. There was some distress, but this Audrey told me they were more worried that they hurt you or scared you than they were worried about a single flower. Flowers bloom and fade, Katie. It's alright."

Katie, still in minor shock that Mary Jane was here, lay back against the hillock. The Audrey leaned over and stroked her cheek with a petal. "I am so sorry!" Katie said, and she wept a while. The petals folded around her cheeks and grew bright and pink and blue where the tears ran.

"We do need to get back soon," Mary Jane said quietly. "We are blessed to be here, but we cannot overstay our welcome. They all need to get on with their days. I'm not sure what they all do, but they do stop whatever it is while we are here." The older woman stood and leaned against the two female Blue Ganeshes. They wrapped trunks around her shoulders. The male held out his trunk to Katie and helped her to her feet.

The baby blue nudged up against Katie. It blew air through the trunk nose section but this time it sounded more like purring. "You called them Ganeshes. Is that really their name?" Katie asked, stroking the baby across the forehead and down between the eyes.

Mary Jane laughed and said, "That is just what I named them. I just called them what they reminded me of when I first came to this place. Like the Audreys made me think of that *Little Shop of Horrors* movie that my boys watch all the time, and the Hindu monkey god is what the flying goo eaters made me think of. Hanumans is a much nicer name than goo eaters, don't you think?

"Anyway, one day a few years back I'd had enough of the noise and chaos at home. You must imagine how it can get. Thank you for always being soft-spoken around me, Katie. You are such a dear. I was hiding in my closet crying and wishing that my kids loved me the way I love them, and then the back wall opened up. I fell through, and here I was.

"The Ganeshes were the first ones to greet me. They wrapped me in their trunks and just held me while I cried. Must have been here for days that first time, but when I went back, the meat loaf hadn't burned or anything. It was like I was never gone. But I felt stronger, more balanced. Especially after the little squidlypusses gave me a massage in the Bathwater Lake. I was scared at first, but everything here just worked so hard to make me feel better."

"Like a spa world?" Katie asked.

"Spa World! I like that! You always know just the right words. You are so smart."

"Why do they do all this, Mary Jane?"

"I think they like us because we care about others. I am always so grateful to be here, and I believe that they are fed by gratitude and kindness. I think that we bring love and appreciation into their world, Katie. I may be rough sometimes, but I just see how to make things happen smoothly. Things get done and people have a good time when someone is in charge, right?"

"Right!" Katie said and reached her hands out to her friend. Her best friend.

They embraced, and that was the strangest thing that happened to Katie all day.

Mars Would Like to Cordially Invite Some Earth Women...

THE FIRST THING SHAWNA NOTICED ABOUT THE ALIEN WAS HOW GOOD IT SMELLED. Something like bread, fresh baked, or maybe oranges, freshly peeled. The next thing she noticed was that it was looming over her bed as she slept.

Residual anger from her divorce and current anger at the cheating ways of Mr. Transition fueled the punch that she hurled at its face. In the dark she couldn't make out any details, but it was rarely completely dark in her room. Amidst the glow of LED clock readouts and the tiny lights of cellphone chargers, computer and monitor switches, and power surge outlets she took aim and connected with the area of the neck. The alien hacked once and then a second time as it fell backwards.

Of course, Shawna did not know it was an alien until she turned the lights on, but in her memory, she could not recall thinking any other way. She rolled from her bed in her tiny studio apartment and snapped on the lights in the small kitchenette.

With her left hand she grabbed the baseball bat she kept next to the bed. *His* bat, a prized possession that she kept out of spite, all the while protesting no knowledge as to its exact whereabouts. "What would I do with a bat?" she asked in all bittersweet innocence. Now she knew. The bat felt wrong in her left hand, but then, she did bat righty.

In her right hand she gripped a squeezable ketchup bottle. The bat she could understand. The ketchup bottle was pure instinct. The studio apartment was so small that the kitchen counter adjoined the bedroom area, and she must have left the condiment out after her dinner of microwave fries and chocolate mint ice cream. And wine. A big goblet and then another. Her love life was stalled, possibly over. Did ketchup go bad if it was kept out in one of those red, squeezy bottles, she wondered?

The alien stood up. Tall and lean and humanoid. Not gray, like in the books and magazines the New Age guy she once dated made her read.

Actually, the alien was a rather pleasant coloring, burnt umber perhaps, with dark curling hair. Except that the hair seemed to move of its own accord. She aimed the ketchup bottle at its eyes and squeezed hard. Shawna had a moment to notice the very nice coloring of its eyes before the red gooey substance connected. A kind of ochre that was a perfect complement to his burnt umber skin tone.

The alien, dazed at her reaction, backed away from the bed. The tiny apartment gave him no place to go. Gathering his wits, he moved towards her, one hand outstretched. It did not occur to her that he may have been reaching out peacefully. Batting lefty, Shawna could only really poke at him. Blinded by the condiment, he did not see the bat to fend it off. The thrust hit him full center of the chest, and he made a noise like Woof! Ketchuped and breathless, the alien fell backwards into a narrow space between the bed and the far wall. He lay very still.

Shawna approached him carefully. As she got near, she saw that his eyes were open amidst the ketchup spray. The alien looked at her but made no moves. She raised the bat and still it did not move.

He spoke. "If I stay very still, will you stop attacking me?" Its voice was pleasant, like a song.

"Who are you?" Shawna was thinking she should be angry, but the words didn't come out that way. She took in the burnt umber coloring, the unnaturally large and quite attractive eyes, the limber limbs with what appeared to be an extra joint, like a double elbow, and sniffing the air, that interesting smell.

Not a cologne. She hated that stuff. It was insecticide to her and repelled her away from men, especially those that were successful and wealthy but apparently preferred artificial pheromones to their own real scent.

No, this quiescent being lying near her bed smelt of, not bread exactly and also not oranges, but close to those and possibly vanilla, but also cinnamon. Or maybe pepper. Smoky spice and strawberry sweet. Maybe. Nothing that would go with ketchup. Suddenly she felt hungry.

Lowering the bat and setting the ketchup bottle aside, she snatched a few old, cold fries remaining on her plate from the previous night. She also glanced at the clock. 4:44. In the morning. Almost time to get up and go to the cubicle farm. Slush piles awaited her attention.

"I take it that the lowering of your ceremonial stick is a sign that I am accepted, if on a limited basis. Is this interpretation true?"

"Are you asking if you can stand up? Yes." She looked at the little table with two tiny chairs, crammed into what the floorplan in the rental office seriously tried to sell as the dining area. "Or sit if you want, but those chairs seem too small for you, string bean. Anyway, what are you? Some *X-Files* thing come to suck my brains out? It'll be a small meal, pal, and mostly mush."

He stood and stretched. In doing so, she heard his joints popping not unlike her own after leaning over a computer all day. He seemed to be taller when finished. Eight-foot ceilings and this guy was a foot away from scrapping his head. The hair moved, but there was no open window to cause a breeze.

"How exactly did you get in here?" Shawna looked at her door and saw the chains and locks still in the on position, the window to the one-foot by three-foot patio still closed and barred. No escape if you were inside. In case of fire, breathe deep and die of smoke inhalation before you felt the flames.

"Here," she said, tossing a dish towel towards him. "Wipe the ketchup off your face with this. Why am I trusting you?"

He did wipe the red goo off. Standing quite still, pondering, or so it seemed, he took his time replying. Thoughtful, thought Shawna. I like that in a man.

"I am named Tellur. Not Stringbee, though if you enjoy that appellation, I will accept it as a nickname. I am not from Earth, but I do believe you have ascertained that fact. I am also not

Exxfilething, but I *am* interested in your brain. Your thoughts, actually, and I do not believe that you are mush at all. In fact, the readings indicate a high level of intelligence, though that does not mean you are required to use it to the highest advantage. Much of your world seems designed to limit the need for..." Again, he pondered, searching for the correct word, "...I believe you say, 'pushing the envelope.' Is that correct?"

"Yeah. Good word choice," she responded, sounding like the editor she was.

"Yes. I was asking if I would or could be allowed to stand up. Gravity here is better dealt with in an upright position. I came through the door with you, but you did not know of my existence. I was not then a part of your reality, so you could not see me. You trust me because I have activated portions of your limbic system that are dormant in many humans and atrophied in most others. It is why you were so effective in defending yourself, as the fight or flight mechanism is now in a better balance. It is less connected to emotional reaction and more to logic. In essence, you will make better decisions under pressure. You will no longer run away from confrontation, physical or emotional. You may also be experiencing what are considered pleasant smells in your personal perception."

"You're an expository kind of guy, aren't you? Thanks for answering my questions in order.

Nice lecture on the limbic system. Why would you do such a thing? Do you just walk about Earth and make people think they are smelling something good, for your own kicks? Is it like a hobby or something? Does no one see you at all? What do you want from me? From Earth?"

"Women."

"What?"

"We want women. For Mars. Or rather, Palinor, as we call our home planet."

"Mars wants women." Shawna's voice was flat, and though she felt puzzled she could not think of a question to ask at that moment. She reverted to what many would assume. "Okay. Prank. This is a prank, right? Someone set this up. Judy? Judy, this has to be you! Come out now. Are you watching me on one of those little spy cameras? Did you hack my computer cam?" She cast her eyes about the room. Computer off. Phone still in her purse. Absolutely no place for anyone to hide.

And Tellur stood patiently against the far wall. Watching and…was he smiling? His mouth was sort of wide but not too inhuman looking to be weird. Slim lips, slim everything really, and long. Long hands, legs, feet, torso, and neck. Only then did Shawna realize he stood there, sans shirt. Muscular, like a basketball player, and she could easily see that he did indeed possess two elbows.

"No prank," he said in his melodic way. Two notes. "No prank," he said, and she knew it to be true. "You are one of a chosen few that have been selected to be invited to return with us to Palinor."

"Chosen few, eh? And what does the selection process involve?"

"Oh, it is vastly improved from the early days. Then we followed a model that we have since learned was imperfect, that of the Hefnerian Philosophy."

"Hefnerian...you mean you read *Playboy*?"

"Yes. The pictures were quite instructional, but I especially enjoyed the structure and style of the writings."

"So, you want me to believe there is magazine delivery service to Mars?"

"What? Oh no, not at all! You see, we once sent envoys to Earth to bring back specimens of Earth women for breeding purposes. That did not work out so well. The guidebooks…"

"*Playboy*."

"Yes, *Playboy* guidebooks were not discovered until we arrived on Earth. The women we located and attempted to take back to Palinor resisted the idea, some of them quite physically."

"You tried to kidnap women?"

"We prefer the term abduct, but yes, your point is well taken. It was all quite barbaric. Those men's magazines seemed to have it all wrong. And aside from the Hefnerian guidebooks, most were poorly written. We decided to lay low for a while and observe to see if a more proper course of action…"

"Like sneaking into my apartment?"

"Er…"

"Okay, so I am some prize winner in the Martian Meets a Maid contest, and you are the messenger. Did I somehow enter this contest, or is it a random drawing? Sponsored by the *Publishers Interstellar Clearing Spacecraft?*"

"Interplanetary."

"What?"

"You said 'interstellar' but that means from the stars, and we only travel between planets. Interplanetary."

Shawna, losing some of her snarkiness at the wider solar systemic concepts being implied, looked first toward her faux patio balcony window and then upward at the ceiling. A closed curtain and an off-white popcorn coating prevented her from seeing the sky, but the gesture of latent awe was noted by the Palinorian.

In a quieter voice Tellur said, "Our initial mission was misguided, if I may understate the situation. We chose to regroup, to pay more attention to words and thoughts than pictures. We chose to seek knowledge and decided to go to the source of femininity.

"We sent a mission to Venus. There we were greeted by an amazing race of beings, beautiful in form, certainly, and we almost abandoned Earth as a source of female genetics."

"But you are here now? Inviting us? Me? Am I supposed to be grateful, even though I am coming in second to the Venus chicks? I gotta tell you, Tellur. You were doing good for a while there, but you may have just lost me."

"Understand that Earth women were our first choice. The Venusians, who call themselves Alluruans, attractive though they may be, are incompatible with our space genetics. One of your scientists discovered this for us, a Dr. Bolen, back in the late 1960s. She too was brilliant and worthy. More worthy than we deserved.

"But the Alluruans are wise beyond the Palinorian male's ability to comprehend. They long foresaw the potential that we would essentially wipe ourselves out due to being too...you have a word for it in your Asian cultures. It is Yang. We on Mars have been too Yang in our approach, and we have burnt out the necessary balancing energies of Yin from our auric fields."

Shawna squinted at him. Was he really the New Age guy in disguise? It certainly sounded like him.

"We have had our consciousness raised. The beings from Jupiter, the ones that live in the upper atmosphere anyway, helped us to become detached from outcomes. The Saturnians helped us see how commitment did not mean restriction of movement. They demonstrated the Ring System, and we Martians realize now that capturing and dominating women is neither necessary nor beneficial for future generations."

"So, Yang is from Mars, Yin is from Venus, Enlightenment is from Jupiter, and Balance is from Saturn? You're going to have to shorten that book title if you want to get on *Oprah*. All this is fine exposition, but what are you doing *here*? Just how long has this mission of yours been going on?"

"My mission is a long one, and we have been here observing Earth societies for several decades. When we arrived there were attempts, botched to be sure, of contacting humanity's leaders. They proved to be dull-witted men, and we moved on to direct contact with women. Our failures were many.

"We retreated to a less inhabited section of the world, a place where we would be unnoticed. A section of Scotland, to be precise, but once we arrived there, we learned that the remnant of women of Mars, my home planet...'

"Called Palinor," Shawna interjected.

"Yes, or Mars to you on Earth. They, the Palinorian women that is, revolted. Revolted against the men, and there was war between the sexes. A female representative from our home planet arrived and attempted to return with male specimens from the Scottish Highlands. It was an excellent choice on her part for they are a hardy, lusty stock, and well suited to survive in the harsher climate of Palinor.

"'Highlanders in Space.' Good Concept. Easy to pitch." Shawna said nodding in thoughtful approval.

"Contact with Palinor was lost for a time. There was that whole Gort and Klaatu incident that disrupted signals…um, well we, the advance team of Martian men, did not know for many Earth years that Palinorian society achieved a balance after the women's revolt. By then we were well integrated in the human world, so long as we did not leave our rural settlements. We felt trapped on Earth at first, alienated as it were, but soon we acclimated to life as fishermen…"

Shawna held up her hand and said, "Okay, that exposition is confusing. It sounds like one too many bad 1950s Sci-Fi drive-in movie plots." Shawna mimicked little scissors snips with her fingers. "So, we edit that part out. And still Earth girls are second best. I do not feel honored simply to have been nominated."

Shawna pulled at her shirt, an oversized, plaid, kind of lumberjack thing that she bought as a gift but kept for herself. Once again, she had fallen asleep in her street clothes. Loose fitting and comfy, they ensured she slept well and saved her from having too much laundry. She called it "her style," but right at this moment she felt frumpy.

She imagined the Alluruans as statuesque, high-breasted and ample, with good birthing hips, or slender and athletic, built for speed and wiry enough to maintain a marathon or decathlon pace. She looked downward at her own torso. Breasts, yes, but hardly ample and at thirty something starting to sag. Too many French fry and ice cream dinners of depression left her more than a little weighty. She felt like soon, if she did not get moving, the sides of her body would flesh outwards like the bodies of her aunt and grandmother. Love handles, they said, but they were both divorced, left for younger, slimmer women. Second best.

"So, what about that subplot, the one with the Palinorian women who passive-aggressively coincidentally invaded Scotland where you, the Palinorian males, happened to have settled? They too were unworthy?"

"Far from it!" Tellur said, eyes widening at the memory. "Nyah was her name, and she was amazing, unlike any Martian woman ever seen before. Statuesque, high-breasted, and dressed in the black Banth leathers generally reserved for warriors. Had she but asked, I would have gone with her, but I realized that she was in need of fresh genetics. Diversity is what is lacking in our world, and if she had chosen me, it would be propagating the same issues that have left us in dire straits."

Shawna felt him winding up to more exposition and held up her hand in a stop motion.

"My question was, 'Why are you here?'" She again pointed to the floor in front of her and spread her arms wide, indicating the narrow apartment and then pointed a finger at her own heart. "Last ditch effort? Am I supposed to be some kind of genetic salvation? Not a goddess to be honored, but cattle to breed new cows to propagate the species? Good word by the way, 'propagate.' Where did you learn English?"

"Game shows mostly. Throughout the solar system we call it the Vanna Effect. Many of the other planetary societies follow closely The Wheel and the Password philosophies. It allows for a rudimentary comprehension of your language…" He trailed off as Shawna began to slowly let her hand rise. "Yes. Well, I wanted to be better, more erudite and began to follow MFA graduates around and read what they wrote. Highly educated, but not always easily accessible. Not so concise. Very wordy."

Shawna glanced at the wall where her MFA certificate hung. This was not going well. "Okay, so you are here on some kind of interspecies, interplanetary, not-so-speedy 2001: A Dating

Odyssey, and I am one of several second-rate sirens that you have mystically chosen to stalk and observe in the night. That is not creepy at all, by the way."

"No? I believed you would be perturbed by my nocturnal presence and..."

"YES! I WAS PETURBED! It *is* creepy! I was scared and might've whacked you to death with my ceremonial trophy from the last-pitched emotional confrontation I avoided by surreptitiously, *sneakily,* passively-aggressively, keeping his damn souvenir sports memorabilia!"

She picked up the bat again and held it in both hands. Raising it above her head, carefully so as not to break the so-called chandelier with the harsh too-bright lights hanging in the not-quite dining area where Tellur now cowered, she advanced on the Palinorian.

"I am not second best! I am not! I am a human doing my best to survive a hard world that does not appreciate my contributions because I *make no goddamn contributions*! I work hard, and someone above me negates my decisions every single damn time! I pick good - *no* - excellent writings from new authors who just want a chance to break into the market. But there is no goddam market! It is all an illusion, and I am a part of the illusion, and I probably don't even exist!" The bat quivered in the air above her head, eye level with Martian.

Tellur lay down on the floor once again, very still. "What are you doing?" Shawna asked.

"I am assuming a submissive position. I desire you to feel your power and value. I believe you exist. Perhaps I am being too straightforward in my explanations and there is some measure of tact missing in my delivery. If so, I do apologize. I am from Palinor. It is our natural way. Certainly, the Alluruans would phrase things in a finer, gentler manner. They speak for a long time before they make a point. It is confusing.

"I only felt that time was of the essence and desired to be direct in my communications with you. No games played. Perhaps some games should be engaged in subtly. Also, I do not want to be struck by such an impressive stick autographed by such a fine athlete as Cal Ripken Jr., a true interplanetary legend of endurance and dedication to duty."

Shawna stood over the Palinorian for a moment, then, lowering the bat, she looked at the writing along the side. She had smudged it. She felt bad. This was something treasured by another human being and, evidently, also by Palinorians and who knew what other species roaming the solar system. In a fit of pique, she smudged that which could not be recovered. She sat in one of the tiny chairs and began to cry.

Tellur stood up and cautiously moved to her side. Gently he loosened the bat from her grip and set it aside just slightly out of her reach. Kneeling beside her, the Palinorian draped his multi-jointed arm about her shoulders. Shawna leaned into his slim, muscular chest. Sobbing, she tried to talk. It all came out as a muffled mess.

"Ah, uh, uh, wan' tabee wanned, y'know? Cherisched and, uh, uh, uhdord! Bu' lookit me! Ma life s'emtee and void. Therse no place fur sumbuddy, uh, uhuh, like me to shine. Whaddaya wa, wah, wan' with me? Go get a Venus chic' fer chrissake!"

"I don't want a Venus chick," he said, and it sounded like a song. "I am inviting you because of all the beings I have ever met, seen, or become aware of, you are the only one that I have ever felt good around. You smell nice to me, and I think I smell nice to you as well. We are compatible genetically, true, but life must be more than that. Relationships are not just living with someone but also living *for* someone. One of our envoys wrote a book about the differences between Martian males and Venusian woman. It is quite popular. Somewhere in the middle are Earthlings, and they are just a little confused sometimes. The Alluruans? Too much for me. Too perfect. Too hotsy-totsy. Is that a word? It doesn't sound right."

Shawna blew her nose on a napkin and said, "Maybe it is a word. Slang for sure, but not quite right. Try 'hoity-toity' and see how that sounds."

"Hoity-toity. Yes, that is the term. Hoity-toity," Tellur said in a high, slightly mocking sound, which shifted to a soft sound like laughter. Like chimes is how Shawna heard it. She snorted a laugh and immediately felt embarrassed.

"Oh, god!" She cried and laughed at the same time. "I have a man from Mars with me, and all I can do is sob and snort! I never sob and snort!"

"I know," Tellur said. He took her face in his other hand, long fingers caressing her cheeks and wiping tears away. "I fear I have been inappropriate in my observations. It has been many years since you came to our attention. We have sensors and instruments all about the earth, but I first noticed your poetry in the college magazine. I read your dissertation on *The Yellow Wallpaper*. It is brilliant. The sense of alienation you expressed, it touched me. I left the other Palinorians and set out to find you. It was not the prescribed way of study, but there was something about you.

"I was going to attempt some subtle form of contact with you in the near future, a letter or phone call, perhaps a request to edit my manuscript, something that would make you feel valuable. But I have fallen in love with you. I hope that you do not mind that I expedited your improved limbic system connection. It is a chemical thing. We have chemistry. That, I believe, is a basis for a relationship. Perhaps we can grow together from here. It is not ideal. But it is true. You are not second choice. I returned from Venus to find you."

Tears were flowing once again. Shawna felt an emotion foreign to her and could not immediately identify it. Then she saw Tellur also possessed tears, large and heavy, hanging just at the corners of those beautiful ochre eyes of his.

"So...am I weak and frail, and you are some big galactic hero come to save the poor hapless serving wench and raise her to interplanetary princess-ness? How long have you been here? How old are you? I mean, I'm okay with winter/spring, but maybe you are pretty late winter. Of course, I'm not exactly spring anymore either. So, okay, winter/summer. How long does a Palinorian live? And what about your friends and family? Will they accept an Earth girl as a...?"

He placed a hand gently near her lips. Not over her mouth. Not forcing her to stop talking. Just...near.

"No. You do not need saving. You are doing fine on your own, only..." He looked at her steadily. "Only perhaps I need you to save me. Perhaps I will perish if I do not live up to my full potential. I can be better. I can learn and grow, but it is difficult for Palinorian males. We live quite long. I am considered young. I want more out of life, and I think that together you and I can be better than we are alone. I can support your dreams, but I do not need to change you.

"The greatest natural resource we have on Mars is Yang. It requires us to be active and do things, but we have lost that which we once did things for. Is that a good sentence? It sounds like a bad sentence. Do you understand what I mean? We lost the Yin creative energy we had with our women when they were around and making us better…That sentence isn't any better, is it?"

"Yeah, let's not diagram sentences just now, okay? I think we are falling in love. Even if you are a creepy stalker alien, I think your heart is in the right place. You weren't going to kidnap me, right? You were never going to force me to do anything I did not want to do, right? In your own way I think you were trying to be honorable, and if it is messed up, well, look at how petty and messed up I am."

Tellur pulled her close, holding her loosely. She could have easily pulled away. She leaned into his chest.

"My heart is placed similar to yours, Shawna." Her pulse quickened when he said her name. "I mean that literally and figuratively. I desire to be valued, and so do you. Valued for who we truly are. On Palinor, we will be. But also on Earth we can make a difference, if we choose.

"We are genetically compatible, and our children will possess certain fresh advantages that the current generation does not carry. It will be difficult for them, and for us, because your militaries do not want the citizens to know for certain that there are other races in the solar system.

"By the way, I could not be a galactic hero, for no one has ever left the solar system. Outside of the orbit of the eleventh planet, there is a mysterious ring we call The Foam that prevents…" His musical words trailed off in slight discord as Shawna looked at him with one side of her face squinched up. She shook her head.

"Too much exposition?" he asked.

She nodded and said, "Start again. Say my name." She put her hand where his heart might be. "Your heart…is this right? My biology is shaky."

"Shawna," he said, placing his hand between her breasts and over her rapidly beating heart. She leaned back, and he leaned in. His wide mouth met her full lips. The tendrils of his hair stroked her temples and intertwined with her hair, holding her close and tight. Biology can be different. Different can be fun.

The sun rose. The day began. Her work cubicle remained empty. The once too small apartment now felt intimate. Shawna and Tellur lay wrapped in each other's arms, peaceful and content. She looked at him and said, "Why me? I am not as beautiful as the Alluruans. My body is not ideal. I am heavy and sagging and…"

He placed a slim finger upon her lips. Her mouth partially open, her tongue at the forefront just behind her teeth, just touching that gentle digit, she paused, gazing into his eyes.

He said, "We can live here or there, Earth or Palinor. On Palinor you will feel lighter. Movement will be easier in the lesser gravity. Things will…perk up."

"Is this some kind of proposal? Are you…?"

"Asking if you will be my bond mate? Yes. But I wish to be sensitive to your needs. Here on Earth is where I first observed you, encountered, came to know and enjoy your skills and talents. I assume that you will wish to remain here. Your career must be important to you. Career is important in many of the novels that women write."

"My career? What is that? Less gravity, you say? How long will it take for us to get to Palinor?"

He smiled a little. "That is humor, yes?"

Shawna raised herself to a sitting position on the bed. Gazing at him in silence for a time. She did not smile exactly, but also she did not frown.

Finally, she said, "This thing that is happening, this story of ours, it is not believable. If I pause too long, I will begin to believe it a dream or some kind of weird seizure. There is no trope here, is there? It is all new and different. No one has ever had a story quite like this, have they? Maybe the 'Scots in Space' guys."

Tellur smiled. Shawna felt the air in the room turn…fizzy with a faint hint of lemon. He said, "It is a story, yes, but does not clearly follow any existing structure. At least not any I have discovered. I do think we have certainly passed the Bechdel Test."

"You know about the Bechedel Test?"

"Yes. It is very useful in more ways than just storytelling. I used it as a guide to building a structure for a potential relationship. You are a woman who easily fits into the milieu described by the test. When you meet with your cubicle mates Alison, Ginger, and Lois after work and swap manuscripts…"

"How do you know we do that? You can't tell anyone we take manuscripts out of the office! They have very strict rules…"

It was Tellur's turn to hold up the hand. "I work at the coffee shop. I hear your conversations. I am a good stalker, yes? But, I promise, harmless."

Shawna moved away from him a bit but remained on the bed.

"When you four speak about the rejected manuscripts, calling them non-commercial, there is respect and sharing in your hearts and brains. When you trade the unmarketable submissions that you personally find to have literary value it is because you desire to share knowledge, true, and the experience of the new, experimental, and different styles of writing that you know will not achieve the pursuit of money the company seeks. You become, not simply slush pile slaves, but the savvy, wise, and singularly intelligent beings you are at your core of existence. You exemplify the Bechdel reality.

"Rule one: At least two women. Rule two: Who talk to each other about... Rule three Something other than a man."

"I often wished I could join in for you are all brilliant and learned. I learned much just from the few things I gleaned while listen..."

"Eavesdropping. Spying. Stalking. That is not the most endearing and romantic thing you might think it is, Tellur. I'm thinking you are kinda proud of all the wrong things."

"I understand that now and accept my error. I believe I have grown. You will, of necessity, be the final judge on my worthiness. This is why I ask you about your statement.

"It is seemingly uncharacteristic of you to be...I risk your ire here, to be so shallow as to desire to abandon Earth for another planet just because of body image.

"I tell you all the things because I wish you to have all I am in front of you, nothing hidden. Of course, there will be things that I forget to bring up and expose. A long life is difficult to sum up. I have taken the liberty to write it all down."

"A manuscript?" she asked in a slightly incredulous tone.

He reached over to her nightstand, small and piled high with books both published and not. From somewhere in the pile, not the bottom, also not the top he pulled a sheaf of pages, not too thick, not too thin.

"It is unsolicited. It is not marketable. It has little chance of becoming a Hall March romance. Or any kind of film, really. It is not commercially viable. My syntax, structure, pacing, are all likely off by a good measure. In other words, it needs work. Just like me."

Shawna slowly turned the pages. Quietly she said, "Mark. Not March. But yes, I don't think we will fit that particular programming format.

"There are some places where there are several blank pages. Otherwise, nice formatting." She paused and lowered the manuscript. "Are you asking me to edit your book? Because that kinda skews the whole 'Come with me to the Casbah and by the way it's on Mars' vibe of the proposal."

Tellur smiled again, and again the air felt fizzy, this time with a scent of lime. "The blank pages are yours. This is your story too. I'm not concerned with anyone editing our life. I'm inviting you, giving you space to fill in your experiences up and to The Now.

This Moment, we begin writing our story together. If you'll have me."

"And there is a publishing house on Mars?" Shawna asked.

"Saturn, actually. The moons, really. One per moon. I'm certain you could get hired if you wish to continue your career."

"Wow. When you give a girl space, you don't mess around. I'll ask again, how long until we get to Palinor?"

In the Blink

SAMMY BLINKED IN THE LIGHT. Not harsh, but bright, and the soft white of the…walls? Was he inside? A woman walked up to him and said, "The jewelry should be divided, but I don't want Anne to get mother's brooch. It should stay in the family. One of the nieces should get that."

Sammy blinked again and wondered what happened to people like this, just wandering about and spouting random things to complete strangers on the…street? The ground was soft and definitely not concrete. White and cushy, but it did not appear to be carpet. Bits of wispy, smoky, tendrils curled up around his feet. He had one shoe on, and the other was missing. It looked stupid. Sammy did not want to look stupid. He took the one shoe off. Certainly, the ground was soft enough to walk on barefoot. The woman wandered off, still talking about the jewelry.

Sammy blinked a third time and looked about, trying to decide if he had been here before. It felt familiar, but…too soon? A man sat in a chair not too far away. It was difficult to gauge distance, for there seemed to be no other physical objects anywhere in sight. He looked back at Sammy and said, "The second quarter is almost over. Can it wait?" He paused as if listening to someone else speaking, but Sammy saw no one other than the older woman. "This game is important. Yes, you are important too, but the garden is going to be under the snow for another two months! We can talk about seeds after the game!" He grew irate. His face reddened and then paled.

Sammy blinked, and the man was no longer there. The jewelry woman likewise had vanished from sight, so Sammy felt there must be some kind of walls or corners where people could disappear from view. But everything sort of ran together, all shades of white. No lines. Nothing to define the world.

"I need to get home and take the garbage out before Mom gets back," Sammy said. He blinked. That was nothing like what he wanted to say. He was going to say, "I think I am lost. I was riding my bike with Allan and Tim, and I think I fell and hurt myself."

The woman he was going to say it to was a nice-looking person with eyes like his teacher. She was older than his teacher and wore loose clothing and a hat. The color of her clothes was…Sammy blinked trying to determine if there was color, but only her blue eyes left the impression of difference from the neutral white shades all about.

Sammy liked the word "neutral." It was one he got in the spelling bee last summer, and it was three grades higher than his own level. He got it right. And then he got the word "origin." Easy! He'd seen that word a million times in comic books. He won on that word because Billy got the word "vacuum" and said, "Double u." The judges disqualified his answer because it sounded like he said, "w."

His teacher had been so proud of Sammy. He was happy that day and studied hard for his spelling and English tests. He studied hard for Miss Bergstrom because he believed she wanted to be proud of him. The woman with the blue eyes reminded him of his teacher, and he wanted to trust her. "My mom told me to get the garbage out this morning before she left for work. I promised her I would. But then I went outside, and Allen and Tim were waiting on their bikes. I don't know if I even locked the door, but I HAVE to get the garbage out, or she will be really angry and not proud."

The blue-eyed woman said, "I don't want to hear it. Take the telegram away. Leave me alone. My chest hurts. It is your fault. No. I won't take the envelope." But Sammy did not see an envelope, and the words he said, that stuff about the garbage, were not important just then, and not what he wanted to say. So why say it?

The blue-eyed woman walked past him after she spoke, and he turned to watch her walk away. By the time he turned she had vanished.

Hat in hand an older man looked at him and said, "It is not the same without her, and I have been here for too long. I will not take the treatments. I will slip away quietly. No one will miss me anyway. I am past being important to anyone. Only Margaret ever loved me. She is gone, and I have no reason to continue. I will not wait for the disease to take me. She is waiting. Maybe. No one will miss me. I will go now." Sammy watched the man fade from view, watched the white light close in upon him.

Sammy hurt a little, and he looked at his hands. They were scraped up pretty badly and looked broken. His arms too. The shirt he wore was torn and red with blood. A woman, young and dressed in white like a nurse, walked to him and smiled. Sammy raised his hands to show her and started to ask for help. "The garbage is really full, and the mice get in if I don't get it taken out. Mom will be so mad if the mice are in the garbage. I just wanted to ride bikes for a little while, but we got to the woods and the creek, and I was having fun, but the garbage is still in the house, and I need to get the garbage out and into the cans in the alley." These were not the words he wanted to say, and the woman in white kept smiling at him, but her eyes were empty.

"So quiet today," she said. "No bombs. No shooting. No casualties. Maybe the war is over? So quiet today."

Sammy's hands did not bleed. They only looked like they should be bleeding. He did hurt when he thought about it, but he did not hurt for long. Like a flash of hurt and then nothing.

No one was near, and he started to say, "Is anyone out there? Can anyone hear me? Where are we?" But he said, "Mom will be home soon, and I have to hurry before she finds out I haven't taken the garbage out to the alley, and the mice will get in the house, and she will be angry like she was at dad before he left. The garbage is the only thing I needed to do today, and I have to hurry and get the garbage out."

And Sammy felt frustrated because he wanted to say, "Where am I?" and have someone answer him and talk to him about the place they were in and say something that made sense to him, but the man now in front of him, just a boy really, but older, said, "Dad will kill me if I wreck the car. I shouldn't be racing Satch and Jimmy. They don't know when to stop. The car is dad's, not mine. I shouldn't be racing."

Perhaps, thought Sammy, if I walk a while, I will find someone to help me. He set off in what he believed might be the direction the blue-eyed woman took, but there was no way to tell. After a short period of time, at least it seemed short, Sammy said out loud, "I am a lost boy! I need some help. Please. Is there a policeman around to help me please?" But the words came out as, "I am a bad boy. I should have taken the garbage out. Mom will be so angry at me."

Sammy did not bother feeling frustrated. No one was listening anyway. No one was ever listening. Mom worked so hard since dad left, and she just went to sleep when she got home. She did not ask him to do much. Just be alone, without her, and be a good boy. Not let anyone in the house and do his chores. The garbage needed to be taken out, and Sammy wanted to do that right now, so badly. He wanted to be home and have his bike in the garage and the garbage out in the alley when his mother came home from the factory and the restaurant.

Sammy wanted to do something nice for her, wanted to be better than he had been recently. He wanted her to look at him and smile again. Not cry. He did not want her to cry. The scrapes on his hands and arms and the torn and bloody shirt would make her cry. It was his only good shirt too.

And the garbage was still in the kitchen, and the mice would get in, and he needed to get home and hurry through the dark streets on his bike. Sammy blinked and walked on into the white light.

The Inevitable
Avocado

I CALL IT THE "CALIFORNIA PROMISE." No, not the one of riches and fame, glory and wealth. Rather the one where they say, "Sure, no problem, we'll be there!" and of course something else becomes more important and they make a noble excuse. Or not. Because no one actually expects to receive a reason for the no-show.

Today the band is good enough, and the songs are familiar enough, and the cause is decent enough that it seems not so many people exercised the California Promise of finding someplace else to be this afternoon. The promoter does not care if people do not show. They paid in advance for their tickets. Fewer people mean less time spent dealing with entertainment and crowd satisfaction.

This is a charity event. We have to support the dolphins. Or the whales. Or the surfers. It always seems to come back to surfing in this town. They even trademarked the term "Surf City" and sought to make a profit on merchandise. I think it backfired somehow. Surfers aren't buying a trademarked phrase for their T-shirt line. Or their custom flip-flops. Or their surfboard wax or... whatever, dude.

Warm air wafts around the outdoor patio at the hotel on the beach. One of the big ones, y'know, starts with H and struggles hard to maintain a beachcomber image while charging massive prices for a room and a meal.

Of course it is not actually on the beach. Pacific Coast Highway runs between the hotel property and Mother Nature's wide repository of sand. Beyond the well-groomed beach is Mother Ocean. Here the waves are regular and not too large. Grommies and Old Guys Who Rule share the cresting waters with the young guns trying to go pro and catch a wave of sponsorship money. The waves are nice here because of the island, or so I have been told. Just twenty-six miles away according to the song. Some days the island is there and some it is not. Today we can see Catalina clear and close as winds are from the desert.

It is a dry heat. Not like Palm Desert, where it gets so hot your ice melts before you can drink your iced tea. Even the famous Starbucks' ice, y'know, that can last all day. Here we have the ocean, and no matter how hot the air is as it arrives, Pacific breezes ameliorate the intensity. This morning, I stepped from my shower and knew we were having a Santa Ana event when I was dry before I touched my towel.

The buffet is being set, and we are listening to the band. Four old guys playing a surf song they wrote fifty years past. Well, only one of them wrote it. Cowrote as it turns out, and there is another band claiming to be the original with the other half of the songwriting duo. They had a fight about copyright and spent more money on lawyers than they ever received from royalties. I am pretty sure they used the law firm that executed the Surf City trademark deal.

I take a picture. That is why I am here. My raison d'être. No one else here would know that phrase.

Of the scheduled celebs only one has shown up - someone famous's son. He has his own radio show, but really, who listens to radio anymore? The guests gather. Fame and fortune. Bump up against it in any form and it might rub off on you. It is all just the illusion of success, but if you can fake it till you make it, other people try to bump up to you.

So the radio-show son-of-a-television-star, who really is pretty nice and fairly witty, gets all the guests' attention until the girl who is famous just for being famous since her nineties youth-oriented cable channel gig arrives and nonchalantly decides to stay when one of her people successfully points her out to a group that is waiting to find someone else who is famous to fawn over without having to wait in line for the radio son. "Hey! Isn't that...?" the assistant says as she stands in a well-lit spot, but out of the too-bright sun. And the crowd squints and says, "Yes. It is her!"

I take a picture of the famous-just-because-she's-famous. I am careful, y'know. Her blond wig is not exactly perfect, her natural dark hair obvious in its escape attempt. I could have snapped a revealing shot that would embarrass her if published. But no one wants to publish that picture of her. It's not like she is a Hollywood big shot waiting to be knocked off her pedestal. She's just a person...trying. Besides, I might make more money from her publicity machine than I would ever make doing the sneak-attack paparazzi thing.

Signaling her attendant, I lean close and say, "I can get some pix for you to use, but you might want to..." I point to my own hairline and pretend to be tucking a wisp under an invisible hairpiece. I am blessed with good hair. The ocean responds nicely and ruffles my blond curls. The attendant takes a moment to gather my meaning, smiling weirdly at me as comprehension dawns on him that I am not propositioning him, and then follows my exaggerated nod and gaze to his mistress's plight. She somehow notes my gaze.

Perhaps it was that the breeze blew my energy her direction. I smile. I am blessed with a good smile. Good teeth. Good facial bone structure. My blue eyes sparkle when I want them to, and at this moment they flash! She returns the favor by turning on her own sparkle. I lean left and take another picture, giving her a quick signal to turn her head to the side that was not faux pas faux hair-ish. I use two fingers instead of one. She gets the message. Employees of the Mouse all understand the two-finger point and I know she was once an employee…I mean cast member…at the Mouse's House. Now she thinks I was also and that makes us familiars. It is a lie I will never need to defend. This will be a good picture. Which, if sold, is also a lie I will never have to defend. But it may get me another gig.

The band is talking about the old days and making surfing references that I do not completely understand, but I listen to them and pick up a few words here and there. You know, "gnarly" and "dude" and such, but that isn't true surf lingo anymore. "Shred." "Tubular." Those still are viable, but it sounds hollow if a landlubber like me tries to use them. The slanguage changes fast and I don't even swim. I respect the culture by not trying to fake it.

Some phrases I really like: "Girl in the Curl" is a good one. I commented to someone that I liked it and that got me a gig as photographer for a book release that covered the whole "real Gidget" crowd. That was fun because some of the women attending were very real and very true. A rare and surprising quality. They weren't promoting anything but the idea that girls, women really, but they said "girls" so I did, too, should be treated equal in all things and surfing was the place to begin. It was a weak argument, but the wine served there was nice, and the pictures were pretty natural. Plus, I got to meet the real Gidget. She's sweet.

My lens finds the one guy in the band who was the writer of the cowritten one-hit wonder, and I move in on him, making myself obvious. He is not as much of a pro at the publicity thing and seems more annoyed at my presence than the famous famous does. I think I "harshed his mellow." At any rate, he seems to be rambling, and his drummer, waiting to perform the famous solo, makes a couple of rolling riffs on the cymbals. It sounds swishy, like the surf, and I switch the direction of the lens to him. He likes it and twirls the sticks. The lead guitarist gets jealous and wants the camera back on him, so he launches into the song. The band, pros and probably studio musicians and not the originals, no matter how tenuous the connection, launch in with nary a pause or dropped beat. And they rock it! I focus on the guitarist's hands as he draws the solo out. Each member has a turn as soloist, just like jazz, but surf beat.

The famous famous makes her way to the front of the patio and does some pose dancing, for which I oblige and shoot a string of provocative shots. Her wig is in place and secure enough, but I note she does not do many head movements. Her assistant stands back, looking chastened and chagrined. He probably delivered the errant hair alarm to her and now is the messenger to be killed.

Taking pix is easy. The crowd never grows unruly. The band grows weary. They are all on social security and Medicare. Probably medical marijuana, too. The buffet opens and I shoot some promo before the artistic layout is demolished by those seeking the free lunch. Of course it is not free, and while people straggle about with their faux fancy plates made of material stiffer than a paper plate but not quite as durable as plastic, and biodegradable, even though trees still were cut down to make the garbage, and petroleum was used to transport the future garbage, and the recycle company does not want the garbage if there was food on it. Still, everyone feels justified about using this disposable dinnerware because the recyclable stamp is clear on the bottom of the future garbage that everyone carries around with their California Cuisine piled high.

California Cuisine—just add an avocado.

The promoter announces the amount of money raised for "the cause," and to be honest, I am not paying attention. The camera is doing its duty, and the promoter will be unhappy with the pictures no matter what. He just does not see himself as an aging surfer. The waxed and styled hipster mustache looks awkward on his fifty-plus, paunchy, balding, faux-Tommy Bahama–shirted body. I can only do so much. I have a good camera.

The famous famous walks past me and says, "I look forward to seeing those pictures you took. Talk to Nigel and he'll give you contact info. He's from England." She turns on her smile once more. I shoot a few close-ups and say thank you. She laughs as if it is funny, and I suppose it is. She does not seem to recognize me at all. It may be some secret agreement. Today we are both VIPs and she is more VI than I.

Nigel is quick to make amends to his mistress and hands me his card, her card, and the company card as if the multitude of paper will secure my personal promise of attention. He says softly, "She wants to see the pictures. I mean she really wants to see your work. But, you understand, only the ones of her." I nod affirmatively. I get the message. Then he actually leans close and whispers, "Her photographer didn't show up." There is real fear in his eyes.

They depart first: So sorry, another engagement: you know how it is when you are in demand, et cetera. The illusion of success. The crowd senses that the party is over and dissipates like the morning marine layer.

The band breaks down their own equipment and the buffet becomes empty after the last stragglers grab "to go" leftovers, of which there is not much. Except for the free wine from the local business. It is awful, but free, and there is a banner that promotes the product. Even surfers have their standards. "Swill," says one as he tastes a dubious pinot grigio from a plastic wineglass. He wears baggies from his own clothing line, and they are pretty nice according to the informal-formal surf dress code. His flip-flops are leather looking, and I recognize them from the display in his store.

He looks at me and smiles in recognition. "Hey, you're the guy from..." and I cut him off, agreeing, but not revealing the secret.

"Yes, I am! How are you? Is your business doing well?"

"It can always be better, but it's all good. I didn't know you do photography. We should talk; I need some promo shots from around the store."

"No worries. I have always liked the store layout and there are some really good pix waiting to happen. I'll even cut you a deal since we know each other." That last bit gets him, but he does like the compliment about the store.

Our social connection is tenuous. Before he can put me off, I say, "Are you in tomorrow? I am off and can stop by any time that is convenient."

His face goes blank. "Sure. Try me tomorrow. I have a few things, but if you catch me in the morning, we can go over some ideas I have." And there it is. The California Promise.

Except I will be there. I want the job. I want the pay. I want to be a photographer and hang out at events where there are famous famous sons and daughters and trust-fund babies. And maybe even get to the point of attending the red-carpet openings with real stars and real cuisine and actual wine that is sold and not given away in the hopes that the little people will see it and buy it for the cheap price and faux prestige.

I am off tomorrow, but the following day I will be back in the produce section stocking the avocados again. Awesome health insurance, a 401(k), and a steady paycheck. The famous girl with the blond wig will come into the store and she will remember where she knows me from. She will be more natural then: no wig, no eye makeup, no need for a photograph. And I will be real with her. I'll speak softly and show her some of the photos and treat her as an equal. We will conspire and maybe she will get me a gig at her next event. Maybe I will get her an invitation to my next photography gig. But no promises. And I will save her some special avocados because she is special and we are both vegan. When it is convenient.

The sun is setting. I take some shots that will be fantastic. But they will look like every other beautiful sunset picture taken from the beach, from the pier, from near the pier, or from pulling over on Pacific Coast Highway. The patio is now empty except for hotel employees acting out their roles. No one is looking at the sunset over the ocean. Why bother? There will always be another perfect day. There will always be another magnificent California sunset over the ocean.

It Happens This Way,
or So I've Been Told

It HAPPENS THIS WAY, OR SO I'VE BEEN TOLD. Sitting staring out the window, watching swirling snow or light rain, trees waving in the breeze or waves rippling across a pond, autumn leaves spinning in the wind or tall grasses swaying in summer fields. Suddenly, imperceptibly, from the corner of the eye…something flits or flutters, a hint of flight or shimmer. You think, "Did I just see that?" You don't believe your own eyes.

Most people get to stop there. They deny the sight, and in doing so deny the gift. They stay within life as they were told it should be; in truth it is the easier course. If you acknowledge what you've seen, or *"what you think you've seen,"* they will say to you, life as you know it goes away.

In my case, it all went away fairly quickly. Fairly early in my life.

The sky was grey. Spring was arriving quite early. Buds appearing on the trees outside my window a full month before the equinox. I sat, depressed, looking out as the snow turned to rain in the late afternoon. "The leaves," I said to myself, "are green."

It was a simple, slightly ridiculous thing to say. "Of course the leaves are green," came the echoing thought. "What color should they be at this time of year?"

To the left, at the bottom of the window, a flash of green, the brightest, greenest of green that I'd ever seen. Or did I see it? I sat very still.

Contemplating the new leaves, I kept my eyes straight ahead. Peripheral vision caught sight of the sudden color, now at the top of the window, looking in.

Looking in?

Eyes?

I sat very still.

She floated down the center of the pane of glass. My breath stopped. My eyes locked open. The silence around increased as my brain shut out all external noise. My body was slack, stunned, and a bit in shock.

"Of course," I thought. "It is simply the pain killers." Having gone to school through the 1960s I knew what a hallucination was, and this must be one now. I had probably taken four pills instead of the recommended two. It was a logical conclusion.

And then she blinked. And then she smiled at me. What could I do? I smiled back. She spun away from the window in a tight spiral, spinning slightly upward into the trees. The feeling of loss was immediate. And almost immediately she slipped back into view. I was filled with joy, a joy that had been absent from my life for so long.

Then the rest of them flew into sight.

I woke up some time later. I had almost convinced myself that it had been an extremely realistic dream brought on by the injudicious use of prescription opiates.

The marks on the window, little smudges that sparkled in the waning afternoon light, caught my attention first. Slowly, with some difficulty, I got out of the large chair where I spent much of my day in recovery. I could see the twigs and leaves outside on the ledge. They were arranged artistically into a smiling face, with one eye winked. The tree debris seemed like it was alive and laughing. I stood staring for a while.

"Perhaps a picture would capture the moment," I thought as I turned to look for my camera. The wind swirled about the window sill, and the face spun off into the air in pieces. I smiled. I winked.

At that point I noticed the pain. It was noticeable because it was not there anymore.

I want to point out to you that this is not an effort to get you to believe anything. In fact, you may have already stopped reading by this time.

It is not an attempt at justifying anything that happened or did not happen after this. It is not an explanation.

It is an invitation.

As the magic came into my life, I had to change. Magic happens in this way, or so I am told. Nothing remains the same once touched by magic. And your life can now change, but you have to believe in magic.

****

I asked you, once upon a time while we were walking in the park, to find fairy hats. Without questioning you bent down and picked up three little acorn caps and said that there must be three fairies nearby. With your usual efficiency, so unusual for a child, you found a place for the fairy hats just off the trail, hanging them off the branch of a plant so that when the fairies returned from playing, they could easily locate their belongings.

Later we played on your favorite bridge and then had ice cream.

Later still, some years later, you asked if fairies were real. "Do *you* believe it?" I asked back. You thought that perhaps they were just a story.

Now I will tell you a story. Maybe you will believe it.

****

After the day of the green leaves, I began taking walks out among the trees. My feeling is that without the glass separating us the little folk were much more cautious about approaching me or allowing themselves to be seen.

They did let me hear them. A chime or slight ringing just behind my head, a brush of wind like the whish of a wing, the sound of a twig bending without breaking. Sometimes it was the absence of noise that became the clue to their presence: a nut dropping from a tree with no landing sound, stepping on a leaf that didn't crunch underfoot. It was all very subtle. And of course, no one would believe any of it, only the very young.

Because of that I became alone, because of magic.

When I saw her again, she flew ahead of us, you and I, on that trail. She was wearing one of the hats you found.

By that time, I had seen many different fairie folk. Had I gone crazy? I would ask myself. The truth was it didn't matter. It was more fun being crazy and seeing the creatures of woodland legend than trying to see the myths of other people. Myths they believed in and devoted their lives to as if true. Myths that I no longer believed as true.

I spent much time enjoying the peace of the forest. Sometimes I would bring cream or honey or sweet nuts, sometime bits of ribbon or string, a sparkle of foil. The purpose of all their activity escaped my human comprehension. It seemed that when I sought to learn a reason, my ability to see them diminished.

So, I stopped looking for reasons. It was the greatest gift.

But the humans around me seemed as if they wanted, more and more, to hear reasons from me. It escaped their ability to understand why I would take the course that I follow. They began to find it hard to see me.

But you always saw. Until the day you asked if it was true.

I wasn't sad that day, although I knew I would miss you. You were always beautiful and now, like so many of us, you had to lose the magic to fit in.

In the future, we humans may not have to go through the process of indoctrination. We may retain the wonder of the universe and be open for the new truths that we learn constantly but notice only occasionally.

She flew ahead of us, waiting to be noticed. Sometimes I think you did see her. It just wasn't accepted that you actually see something like a fairy. You would stop, gaze a bit, turn and look at me for approval.

She seems to be the ambassador to humanity. She likes us. She provides us with a friendly introduction. She beckons us to follow, for there are great gifts that we can learn from the elementals of planet earth. She will not tug or pull or drag us to the realm of reality that we call magic. She only invites us.

I see her still and often. I see her companions as well. I see the green of the earth and the blue of sea. Now I do what I can to give people space to believe. It is difficult for humans. We are well trained in the ways of blindness.

The invitation never ends. Sight can be restored. Perhaps we will walk together again, you and I.

It wasn't up to me to give you approval on your reality. It is up to you to create your reality.

It always happens this way...

The End of Your World as You Know It

I KNOW THE EXACT WEEK THAT YOUR WORLD ENDED and mine began. I have a good idea of the exact day. Your newspapers stop at a specific point. They are filled with tales of what to do in the face of disaster. Some become filled with fear. Others make attempts to remain practical. One appears to be taken over by zealots from one of your many religions. Their god did not heed their pleas.

Nearly every source of information indicates a belief that civilization would resume. All speak of a moment when things become "normal" again. Your "normal" no longer exists. Normal is now. My normal.

We, the survivors of your disaster, still do not know what exactly happened. A plague of some sort, certainly, but there was more, wasn't there?

Outbreaks of violence were reported, but it was more than mere terrorist attacks. Some serious weapons were involved. Some serious damage was inflicted. Did you do this to yourselves? To all of us? We see from your records that you built the machines. You knew of the destructive power. What did you hope to gain?

We see the remnants of Experiment IV. Sound intensification as a weapon. Why? How could you imagine such a thing? The ruins of the complex are clearly labeled. Were there more? Experiments I through III? More? How many of them were there? Are they all based on the senses? Destruction with light intensification, or the sense of smell? A thought experiment? Did you release their energies all at once?

Experiment IV looks to have destroyed itself as well as much of the surrounding area. We see the scars of it all still. Much is overgrown, and the earth heals itself.

Are you the ones that made the craters? We have motion pictures of you doing just that on a small scale all over the world long before those last weeks. We do not understand the logic behind such action. Craters still exist, but after nearly two hundred years they look more like valleys. Some retain water, becoming lakes. I take my children fishing in one of them. We eat well.

It may disturb you to know that we don't particularly care *what* happened. We care *why* it happened. Those that lived through the hard times had enough to do just surviving, just preparing for their future. It is only recently, in my lifetime, at this point in our development, that we have the time to examine the old records for clues and hints. We wish to avoid the mistakes made by you.

We know about television. We have sampled many shows from the 20th and 21st Centuries. Did you really find importance in all those diversions? Did it really entertain you to see the gruesome crimes you committed against one another?

Was *this* your normal? Amused by death?

So many relics of your world survive. So much waste. We are curious. We are also cautious. You frighten us. You had so much. Why did you fight? Why did you horde? Why could you not share with one another?

We see the fear and loneliness on your faces. We see it growing as time goes on. Didn't you see that you were isolating yourselves, separating from one another, and weakening the entire web of vitality that linked you to the planet earth?

Did you not *see* each other?

We are like you in one respect. We are fascinated by the past, by what went before and the way you lived. There are many existing historical records. You kept meticulous details of the last centuries and made great inroads into an understanding of what went before. It appears, from my first overviews, that you often had an agenda in doing so.

You seemed to be wanting, always, to prove something about yourselves. You appear to have needed to be absolutely right about something. You sought to be superior to those of the past. In so doing, you often sought to prove others completely wrong.

It may interest you to know that we no longer follow any of your beliefs. It isn't that we ban them; it is that we have no need for such convoluted mythologies. The cycles of life on Earth are wonderful enough. The sky above holds enough beauty that we do not feel the necessity to invent beings of unearthly glories. In this we have no reason to fight about which god is a better god. This seems so important to you. From my studies, few of you acted in ways that your gods instructed, especially at the end of your world.

End Communication One

****

Three good beings guided humanity after that, your era. They first pointed out that, as there were so few humans left, there was a greater need to co-operate than to defend. Looting was unnecessary. There was enough stored water and clothing in distribution centers, what you called stores, to go around. Shelters were plentiful. So many dwellings were left abandoned, intact. Much of the destruction of humanity was biological and not physical.

Wind turbines and solar panels still exist. Warehouses full of technologies are being discovered. Archives of technical journals are carefully preserved. Stan Welles, one of the three guides, immediately set up education centers. He knew how to teach, but he also knew *what* to teach. His first priority was securing our heritage of learnings.

After the shift one of the first wisdoms was to maintain your libraries. We searched for other collections of knowledge, technological records and the like, coalescing the contents and bringing all closer to us. It is not that all you learned was wrong. So much knowledge and not enough wonder. We use this knowledge now and do not seek to profit individually. So many technologies were available to you, so many solutions. Again, we ask, why was there hunger, why disease? Why was there poverty?

Esther Powell, Aunt Esther we call her, she knew planting and seasons. She knew water. She knew hydroponics. We exist in this southwestern desert still through her guidance. The weather is pleasant in the southern and western parts of what you knew as America. We live at the edge of the water. We live with the land and do not seek to control it, save for agricultural use. The Pacific Ocean still surges. Humans still ride her waves.

We are different from you. What afflicted you, what killed you, made us stronger. We feel it made us better than you ever could have been in that overcrowded world you tried to live in.

Didn't you sense it? Didn't you feel the intensifying pressures? Did you not suspect that the rising rates of diseases were due to the strange hyper-intensive lifestyles you imposed upon yourselves?

We are better, but you could have been us.

End Communication Two

****

Life is problem solving. You seemed to believe that life was conflict. We still have stockpiles of your weapons and use them from time to time. We do not think of them as weapons. We believe they are tools to be used responsibly and with specific purpose. Build up society, not destroy others.

In your communication to us you asked the question, "Did the gun nuts win?" We see who you are by this question.

Nobody won. The strong did not survive. The meek did not inherit the earth.

Immediately after the shift, there remained some who sought to merely take from others, rather than share. Remnants of your time who chose to fear rather than hope.

Our community was involved in two great conflicts. Not as extensive as your world wars nor even as the smaller disputes you called skirmishes. Local battles. A repelling of men who sought to control others, rule and dictate. It is a relic, the thought of a class of men who rules over others who then must serve.

We do not tell of those days of discord with pride. There are no grand memorials to the sacrifice of youth, no honoring dying or death dealing. We do not make parades and set days aside in honor of these battles. We speak of them and ask: What could have been done to avoid bloodshed and death?

Dane Powell, Aunt Esther's only child, put down the principles by which we live today. We need very few laws because of them:

Seek ways to keep others healthy.

Seek ways to share.

Walk on.

End Communication Three

****

The final days of your world must have been horrific. If you possessed a cure for what seems to be multiple plagues and epidemics, you still would not have been able to stop the natural disasters that occurred, will occur, shortly after. There are some now who believe you caused them. Perhaps inadvertently. Perhaps not.

In our day, there are few children. Possibly the physical things that affected you also changed us in some way. We do not procreate easily. A level of population is maintained.

There is much thought and energy put into bringing a child into the community. You seem to have produced babies without any thought at all. We believe this weakened the species immensely. And now, you are not here.

It was the children and the elderly that went first. Reports say they simply stopped moving, slumping to the floors or just passing away where they sat. Once started, the deaths moved in circular patterns throughout the country and the world. We do not know how extensive this death spiral was, but all the world reported the event at the beginning.

Fear gripped the governments early. Each blaming another. As I research, I see that fear was often a motivation for the action of the governments and the population of the planet.

The earthquakes you feared, occurred. The Mighty Three were magnificent events. Those that lived through them recall with awe the power of the earth. Over a period of seventy years the land and coastlines are radically reshaped. Had you been alive in your great numbers there would have been much loss of life and property.

No doubt your leaders would have said things like, "Our prayers are with you," and other meaningless words. The records show these things were spoken a lot. The records do not show a pure agenda of assistance. Sometimes there is no record of assistance at all.

After each individual quake, we sent emissaries and rescue parties into affected communities. We helped rebuild and brought supplies. After the first devastating event, our society came to rely less on processed goods and more on living off the land. Recovery is easier when the destruction is minimized. If need arises, we adapt and supply so that all are warm and well fed.

And we teach.

Borders vanished. Our populations merged, no single race or ethnic branch taking a superior position. We are all in the same situation. We all seek to improve our lot. Cooperation brings stability. The earth is rich and fertile. There is plenty for all.

A traveler, a man of the sea, arrived one day. He spoke to me of the world as it is now. It was not only the quakes in our vicinity. There was more. He spoke of, indeed displayed maps he drew of the area once called the Mediterranean Sea. He now labels it the Saharan Ocean. What was once desert is now a vast expanse of water with lush coasts of jungled life. Green and blue and vibrant.

The strike of a rock from outside earth's atmosphere decimated what were once thriving civilizations to the north and east of the vanished desert.

Those days will be fiercely difficult for you to live through.

I wonder, were the weapons you used an attempt to divert destruction? Did they only get out of control and their use was not against one political entity by another?

If my theory is true, it must happen late in the Era of Destruction for there are no records of such thinking.

In this region the traveler describes, humans do remain, reduced in number, living close to the land. Much like we exist here today. He speaks of them with respect. They too choose cooperation and peace, for what reason do they have to quarrel? I hope to see him again one day, and soon, for I enjoyed his smile.

End Communication Four
****

We have found your machine. It is brilliant in its design, and you were correct to use the power of the sun. It is what kept the construct active and, for the most part, well-maintained. The directions are simple. The machine works from our end. The energy required to power your communicating device is used up rapidly with each session. It replenishes slowly. Thus, we keep our communications brief.

Though we had hints, clues, and even some basic instructions, it took us some time to unseal the vault. As I have said, we are cautious about things that you built. It has taken us more time to decide to use this tool, Experiment V.

What was your original intention? What prompted you to spend such time and resources building a device that would communicate in one direction only? Were you communicating with someone in *your* past, sending messages back, just as I am doing now? We see no evidence of this.

You apparently planned on receiving communications from your future. Why else make such an effort? Is that the sole reason for this machine? What a remarkable project for a society that devoted so much time to preserving the past. Or was that the goal? To find a way to preserve yourselves? Or worse. Was it an attempt to profit?

Prior to your world's end, well-meaning scientists wrote questions to us. I have the notebook in front of me now. You were very specific in seeking information and outcomes. You asked bright questions that would give you foreknowledge of the events that must already be in progress in your time. We, here in your future, are cautious about using your Experiment V. We cannot predict the outcome of taking this action, but we have chosen to send this message anyway. When finished, we will seal this vault once more.

End Communication Five

****

We will not grant you information that may change the outcome of your future, my present. The population of Earth suffered already. If you change your present, your future, *my* past, will we be doomed to suffer again? More?

The ramifications of time travel are too weighty to be trifled with, and we do not wish to engage in ethical debate regarding any attempt to rescue you. What happened happened and the end result is fine with us.

Our world is better.

You see, the answers we might offer will not improve the way things are in my present day. You were granted many opportunities to alter your course. You are stuck in your ways. You cling to and defend traditions that long ago ceased serving the community of the globe.

Even your keyboard arrangement is archaic with the letters scattered about in no clear order. It is simple things like this that baffle us. We sometimes feel no recourse but to laugh at your beliefs, but we always remember what the consequences were. It is sobering to ponder the extent that you, all of you, went to defend and impose ideologies.

If you receive this message, then you will know that the human race did not simply survive. We thrive. We seek growth. We are at peace, but only because we reject so much of what you found precious.

The earth is not a wasteland. Despite your efforts, your activities did not destroy it. The planet is mighty and heals itself over and over in vast creative ways. We model our society after the actions of the earth.

We do not love you. Nor do we hate you. You are not honored. You are not considered the pinnacle of civilization. You are studied. In the same way that you looked at other cultures from the past, we look at you. There is a difference.

We do not impose our personal moral code upon you. We do not look at what may be considered inferiorities or mistakes of the past to prove our personal vision of correctness. We witness your patterns and use them as examples. What brought consequences of growth? What brought consequences of ruin?

There is no judgment sought. Only lessons to benefit ourselves.

We do not look to you that often.

End Communication Six

****

You ask about your children. You ask if certain family lines survived. We feel that you ask out of a sense of pride. We feel that you are seeking a status of superiority. It may be better for you to be comfortable within your own actions. This is a common problem with your society. You so often seek validation outside of your own thoughts and feelings. Why could you not be content with your own lives and the results of your personal actions?

We found this machine. Experiment V? Time travel? You were so ambitious! But time travel by information transference only, we assume.

We found two of the five maintenance robots still working. We also found Joseph.

He made himself comfortable in his last days. He wrote out his story. He left pictures of his family and children. He had sent them away from the city. He did this out of love. He remained out of a sense of duty.

He is the one who appears to have activated all the equipment here. He watched you all. He was proud of his menial work. But he was a smarter man than you bothered to understand. He learned, though you never taught. And in the depths of night, he planned.

Sometime, in those last days, he allowed himself to be sealed within this vault. He knew it to be his tomb. You were not around to operate the equipment. You all fled.

He remained behind, pressing buttons in the sequences he had observed while cleaning your broad windows, sterilizing your bright floors, and polishing your gleaming walls. On that last day he took out your trash, brought the last of his supplies inside, and pressed the final buttons, sealing himself within and you without.

Joseph is the liaison between my past and your future. I know he is receiving these messages for he wrote out the dates and times and noted specific settings that would allow us to communicate with him alone.

In his notes, he sent his love to his family and any grandchildren or great-grandchildren that might follow. Mostly he sent his love to his wife, with the reminder that they came to this country to make a better world for themselves and their children. He believed that a better world was possible, but the society he lived in must first come apart.

If we have timed this correctly, he will be on duty when this message arrives. The machine will come alive, and he will see our words printing out.

The shift will have begun. The death spiral will be well under way. This message will be transferred to the leaders of the world and the controllers of the project from within the sealed vault where only the maintenance man remains. We will not know if we succeed for there is no follow-up communication from him. Your aging machine is failing. We have no technology to repair it.

Take comfort, Joseph. We found you because your beloved wife kept her journal in detail, with her children and yours adding to it and passing it down through the generations, decade by decade. She survived in the remote community in the hills, the one I myself lead and guide today. She lived well and kept your memory faithfully.

Joseph, my great, great, great, great grandfather, thank you. You are well loved by your family to this day. I will give birth to yet another generation, and the world is a good one.

The earth is a beautiful planet.
It is not always a safe one.

End Communication from the Future
****

JEFFREY J. MICHAELS IS A GEMINI. As such he is deeply involved in whatever interests him at the moment.

He describes his short story collections, *Angel of Reality and Other Unorthodox Encounters* and *A Day at the Beach and Other Brief Diversions* as "metaphyictional," combining fantasy and humor with metaphysical elements.

He is currently polishing a sweeping fantasy series of interconnected tales collectively known as The Mystical Histories. It is varied enough that he says he may even finish most of the stories.

Book One of Tasa's Passage Trilogy, *Tasa's Path*, is available on Amazon. Book Two, *Tasa's Journey*, will be published soon. You may also enjoy the short tale introducing Jack A'the Green, *Crossing Jack*, also available on Amazon.

In Jeff's real life he is a well-respected creative and spiritual consultant. He does not like to talk about his award-winning horror story.

You can visit him at www.jeffreyjmichaels.com